OXFORD STUD

Series Editor: Steven Croft

Emily Dickinson

Selected Poems

Edited by Jackie Moore

Consultant: Victor Lee

Oxford University Press

OXFORD
UNIVERSITY PRESS

Great Clarendon Street, Oxford OX2 6DP

Oxford University Press is a department of the University of Oxford.
It furthers the University's objective of excellence in research, scholarship,
and education by publishing worldwide in

Oxford New York

Auckland Cape Town Dar es Salaam Hong Kong Karachi
Kuala Lumpur Madrid Melbourne Mexico City Nairobi
New Delhi Shanghai Taipei Toronto

With offices in

Argentina Austria Brazil Chile Czech Republic France Greece
Guatemala Hungary Italy Japan South Korea Poland Portugal
Singapore Switzerland Thailand Turkey Ukraine Vietnam

Oxford is a registered trade mark of Oxford University Press
in the UK and in certain other countries

First published in 2006

British Library Cataloguing in Publication Data
Data available

ISBN-13: 978-019-832545 1
ISBN-10: 0-19-832545-2

10 9 8 7 6 5 4 3 2 1

Typeset in Goudy Old Style MT
by Palimpsest Book Production Limited, Grangemouth, Stirlingshire

Printed in Great Britain by Cox and Wyman Ltd., Reading

The publishers would like to thank the following for permission to reproduce
photographs: P2 Yale University Digital Images; p4 Yale University Digital Images;
p6t James Marshall/Corbis UK Ltd; p6b Yale University Digital Images; p142 Yale
University Digital Images; p144 Hulton Deutsch Collection/Corbis UK Ltd; p150
Bettmann Corbis UK Ltd; p183 Yale University Digital Images

Contents

Acknowledgements v

Foreword vi

Emily Dickinson in Context 1

Selected Poems of Emily Dickinson 11

67 Success is counted sweetest 11
79 Going to Heaven! 11
199 I'm 'wife' – I've finished that 12
211 Come slowly – Eden! 12
213 Did the Harebell loose her girdle 13
214 I taste a liquor never brewed 13
216 Safe in their Alabaster Chambers 14
249 Wild Nights – Wild Nights! 15
254 'Hope' is the thing with feathers 15
258 There's a certain Slant of light 16
280 I felt a Funeral, in my Brain 16
288 I'm Nobody! Who are you? 17
303 The Soul selects her own Society 17
315 He fumbles at your Soul 18
322 There came a Day at Summer's full 18
327 Before I got my eye put out 20
328 A Bird came down the Walk 20
341 After great pain, a formal feeling comes 21
401 What Soft – Cherubic Creatures 22
414 'Twas like a Maelstrom, with a notch 22
441 This is my letter to the World 23
444 It feels a shame to be Alive 23
446 I showed her Heights she never saw 24
465 I heard a Fly buzz – when I died 24
501 This World is not Conclusion 25
510 It was not Death, for I stood up 26
512 The Soul has Bandaged moments 27
528 Mine – by the Right of the White Election! 28
585 I like to see it lap the Miles 28
640 I cannot live with You 29

657 I dwell in Possibility 30
663 Again – his voice is at the door 31
668 'Nature' is what we see 32
670 One need not be a Chamber – to be Haunted 32
690 Victory comes late 33
709 Publication – is the Auction 34
712 Because I could not stop for Death 34
732 She rose to His Requirement – dropt 35
741 Drama's Vitallest Expression is the Common Day 36
747 It dropped so low – in my Regard 36
754 My Life had stood – a Loaded Gun 36
986 A narrow Fellow in the Grass 37
1068 Further in Summer than the Birds 38
1072 Title divine – is mine! 39
1100 The last Night that She lived 39
1129 Tell all the Truth but tell it slant 40
1138 A Spider sewed at Night 41
1183 Step lightly on this narrow spot 41
1263 There is no Frigate like a Book 42
1286 I thought that nature was enough 42
1551 Those – dying then 42
1670 In Winter in my Room 43

Notes 45

Interpretations 135
Ideas and influences in Dickinson's poetry 135
Themes in Dickinson's poetry 152
Language and style 173
Critical history 182

Essay Questions 187

Chronology 190

Further Reading 194

Glossary 196

Appendix 202

Acknowledgements

The poems are taken from *The Poems of Emily Dickinson* edited by Thomas H. Johnson (The Belknap Press of Harvard University Press, Cambridge, Mass.), copyright © 1951, 1955, 1979, 1983 by the President and Fellows of Harvard College, reprinted by permission of the publishers and the Trustees of Amherst College.

Acknowledgements from Jackie Moore

I would like to thank Steven Croft for his clear guidance and constant support. I am grateful to Jan Doorly, who has edited this text with her usual sensitivity and intuition. I am also indebted to a friend and colleague, Paul Dean, with whom I have had many stimulating discussions about this poetry. Finally, I would like to thank all at OUP who have helped to bring this project to fruition.

Editors

Steven Croft, the series editor, holds degrees from Leeds and Sheffield universities. He has taught at secondary and tertiary level and is currently head of the Department of English and Humanities in a tertiary college. He has 25 years' examining experience at A level and is currently a Principal Examiner for English. He has written several books on teaching English at A level, and his publications for Oxford University Press include *Literature, Criticism and Style*, *Success in AQA Language and Literature* and *Exploring Language and Literature*.

Jackie Moore read English at Manchester University with American Literature as a specialism. She was later awarded her doctorate in English with Philosophy. After lecturing on American literature in higher education, she moved to the secondary sector, becoming head of an English department. She is now an educational consultant and Senior Examiner in A level English literature.

Foreword

Oxford Student Texts, under the founding editorship of Victor Lee, have established a reputation for presenting literary texts to students in both a scholarly and an accessible way. The new editions aim to build on this successful approach. They have been written to help students, particularly those studying English literature for AS or A level, to develop an increased understanding of their texts. Each volume in the series, which covers a selection of key poetry and drama texts, consists of four main sections which link together to provide an integrated approach to the study of the text.

The first part provides important background information about the writer, his or her times and the factors that played an important part in shaping the work. This discussion sets the work in context and explores some key contextual factors.

This section is followed by the poetry or play itself. The text is presented without accompanying notes so that students can engage with it on their own terms without the influence of secondary ideas. To encourage this approach, the Notes are placed in the third section, immediately following the text. The Notes provide explanations of particular words, phrases, images, allusions and so forth, to help students gain a full understanding of the text. They also raise questions or highlight particular issues or ideas which are important to consider when arriving at interpretations.

The fourth section, Interpretations, goes on to discuss a range of issues in more detail. This involves an examination of the influence of contextual factors as well as looking at such aspects as language and style, and various critical views or interpretations. A range of activities for students to carry out, together with discussions as to how these might be approached, are integrated into this section.

At the end of each volume there is a selection of Essay Questions, a Further Reading list and, where appropriate, a Glossary.

We hope you enjoy reading this text and working with these supporting materials, and wish you every success in your studies.

Steven Croft *Series Editor*

Emily Dickinson in Context

Dickinson and her home

Emily Dickinson was born in 1830 in Amherst, a pleasant, though rather old-fashioned, rural town. Her family was genteel and quite wealthy; she had a brother, Austin, who was one year older than herself, and a younger sister Lavinia born in 1833. The family had earlier experienced financial difficulties, but by 1855 her father, Edward, was able to buy back the elegant house 'The Homestead' which her grandfather had built, and to build a spacious house next door, 'The Evergreens', for his son and daughter-in-law Susan Huntington Gilbert.

Emily Dickinson's father was a prominent citizen of Amherst; he was a lawyer, trustee of Amherst Academy and treasurer of Amherst College, both of which her grandfather had helped found; he was on the committee of Amherst First Church, and a politician locally and also at one time for the US Congress. Because of his connections, The Homestead was often visited by influential guests such as judges, politicians, church ministers and newspaper editors. Her mother, Emily Norcross Dickinson, was frail and timid, and increasingly invalided; Emily Dickinson felt that she had 'no mother', and along with her sister Lavinia was obliged to run the household shortly after the move to The Homestead.

Her father believed in educating girls, so Emily attended Amherst Academy until 1847, when she moved on to Mount Holyoke Female Seminary. This college had a religious curriculum, but Emily Dickinson had too many grave doubts to commit to Puritanism and was called a 'no-hoper'. She left early, in 1848. She was familiar with much great literature including Shakespeare, the Brownings, Keats, George Eliot and Americans such as Ralph Waldo Emerson, Walt Whitman and Nathaniel Hawthorne.

Emily Dickinson, in about 1848

Emily's sister Lavinia Dickinson, in the 1850s

Emily Dickinson commented that Amherst was 'alive with fun' in 1849–1850, and she seems to have enjoyed society at her brother's home in 1858. But she became increasingly isolated; first she refused to visit an old friend in 1854; then in 1860 she made her last social visit away from home, aged 30. She refused to travel even to visit her friend and mentor Thomas Higginson, and after 1860 she went only twice away from home for treatment on her eyes, when she feared that she was losing her sight, in 1864 and 1865.

In September 1861 she had suffered a 'terror'; no one is sure exactly what happened, but perhaps she had mental health problems connected with the fear of losing her eyesight. There are many references in her poetry to terrible mental trauma. She became a recluse, took to wearing white dresses and perhaps became agoraphobic (afraid to go out); however, she kept in touch with family and friends through her many letters, often including poems or poetic fragments. She died in 1886, either of kidney disease or of a heart attack caused by hypertension.

Dickinson and love

It is known that Emily Dickinson was a passionate woman who experienced several love affairs. Commentators debate whether she was heterosexual, bisexual, to some degree a lesbian or perhaps auto-erotic. Her greatest love affair appears to have been with her best friend Sue Gilbert, to whom in 1852 she wrote a moving love letter. It seems that this passionate love was not reciprocated; seeing Sue fall in love with her brother Austin, Emily Dickinson helped them to become engaged. This may have caused her considerable pain; for the year after they married, in 1856, there are few details of her life.

She also had male friends, including several close relationships. The first, 1850–1853, was with one of her father's law clerks, Benjamin Franklin Newton; he gave her a copy of

Susan Gilbert Dickinson, the poet's friend and later sister-in-law, in about 1850

Austin Dickinson, the poet's brother

Emerson's poetry and she called him her 'tutor'. It is also suggested that there may have been a relationship with a dynamic young married clergyman, Reverend Charles Wadsworth, whom she had met in Philadelphia in 1855, with whom she corresponded, and who visited her twice. There is also speculation about an affair with a local newspaper editor, Samuel Bowles. However, it is certain that her relationship in 1878–1882 with an older man, Judge Otis Lord, concluded in a proposal of marriage which she declined. Three letters of 1858, 1861, and 1862 were found addressed to 'Master', but it is not known to whom these letters were sent, if indeed they were ever sent at all.

There is much evidence of her passions in her poetry, but Emily Dickinson was troubled by the subordinate and inferior role of women in contemporary society; she perhaps felt that marriage made their limited status even weaker, and there are many poems that consider this problem. In this sense, her refusal to conform to society's expectations about marriage, instead choosing social withdrawal, could have been partly a gesture of defiance.

Dickinson and her poetry

Emily Dickinson began to write poetry when she was young, and her first known poem of 1849 is a 'comic valentine'; however, her work was developed by a man who was to become a life-long friend, visiting the poet several times. In 1862 she read an article in the April edition of *Atlantic Monthly* by Thomas Higginson about the power of poetry and responded, including copies of four of her poems. Interestingly, she adopted the pose of a naïve young girl who had not yet started to write (she experiments with adopting poses and personae throughout her poetry). In fact, she carefully explained to Higginson that the 'I' in her poems was not herself but a 'supposed person'. She was unwilling to go into print, and indeed Higginson advised her not to. Instead, she sent

'The Homestead' in Amherst, Massachusetts, built by Emily Dickinson's grandfather

The Dickinson family; silhouette from 1847 or 1848

her poems to friends and family and from 1858 began to sew the poems into little books called 'fascicles'. In her lifetime she published perhaps a dozen poems; but on her death her sister Lavinia found what amounted to almost 1,800 poems.

Dickinson and her society

Despite her comfortable family background, Emily Dickinson lived at a period of great social change. New England was the centre of intellectual life in America, but was still conservative (it had been the landing place of the Pilgrim Fathers who brought Puritanism to America). Religious tradition in Amherst had been strong, but these beliefs were being challenged by new thinkers such as Charles Darwin with his theory of evolution, and philosopher–poets such as Emerson and Whitman, who undermined traditional belief in the existence of God with their Transcendentalism. Emily Dickinson studied these writers and admitted the value of their ideas; she could not commit to traditional religious views.

Social change was also evident as the older, aristocratic type of society in New England was being undermined by the Civil War, which was tearing American society apart. There was unrest with the civil rights movement, problems derived from slavery, and protests about women's rights provoked by the inferior roles women played in society. Even the coming of the great railway to Amherst – another of her father's causes – suggested that society would change, becoming more mobile and democratic.

Unlike her siblings, Emily Dickinson could not accept the old ways of her society so she withdrew into her home and her room; her withdrawal could have been the result of illness, a retreat from unstoppable social change, a rebellion against the subordinate roles of women in her society, or quite possibly the only way in which she could dedicate herself wholly to her vocation as a poet. A sense of crisis is evident throughout her poetry, in which she probes and challenges issues of faith and doubt, of social crisis, of life and death. She frequently weighs up the balance between conflicting viewpoints, seeking to explore ideas rather than to find solutions. Often her poems end with the two opposite positions finding no reconciliation, or in one cancelling out the other in stalemate. It is often this conflict that is the dynamic force driving her poetry along.

To the student of today, perhaps the most attractive quality of Emily Dickinson's poetry is that she is a rebel against many 'normal' attitudes to the religion, society and culture of her time. To express her rebellion she wrenches and twists the rules of language, making it something strenuous and quite shocking. In these ways she is truly modern, so her poetry will speak to all students who care to listen to her voice.

Contexts in Dickinson's poetry

From this brief biography you will see the contexts in which Emily Dickinson's poetry was established. There are many possible contextual routes to understanding of her poetry; here are eleven examples.

1. Against the background of the outbreak of the American Civil War, and much political engagement in her household, there are poems that explore the contexts of **war and politics** – for example 67: *'Success is counted sweetest'* and 690: *'Victory comes late'*.
2. As her letters show, Emily Dickinson often made mocking comments on the social customs and pretensions of contemporary society, and this is seen in her poetry in **satires and comments upon society** – for example in 401: *'What Soft – Cherubic Creatures'* and 585: *'I like to see it lap the Miles'*.
3. Amherst was a pretty little rural town, and it is obvious in

some of her poetry that she appreciated its beauty; however, Dickinson generally moved beyond mere praise in her poems about **nature**. Examples are 258: *'There's a certain Slant of light'* and 986: *'A narrow Fellow in the Grass'*.

4 Emily Dickinson obviously experienced great passions, and this is evident in her poems about **love and sex** – for example in 249: *'Wild Nights – Wild Nights!'* and 446: *'I showed her Heights she never saw'*. She also wrote about **different types of love**, such as that between an individual and the community, the reciprocal love and consideration that should follow loyalty, and love of our fellow human beings. She is a poet of compassion.

5 Her concerns about women in society were evident in her poems about **marriage**, for example in 199: *'I'm "wife" – I've finished that'* and 322: *'There came a Day at Summer's full'*.

6 Living in an age of fairly strong Puritanism, but seeing the deaths of friends and acquaintances in the dreadful Civil War, she wrote many poems about **death and immortality** – for example 465: *'I heard a Fly buzz – when I died'* and 1100: *'The last Night that She lived'*.

7 Her religious doubts were evident when Emily Dickinson left her seminary after only one year; she was tortured by doubts as to whether God was just; whether there really was redemption and salvation; even whether there was a God at all. Her debates are evident in her poems on **religion**. Some examples are 315: *'He fumbles at your Soul'*, 510: *'It was not Death, for I stood up'*, and 1551: *'Those – dying then'*.

8 Her concerns about social injustice for women may also be at the heart of her dramatic monologues and poems about **gender issues**. Throughout her life Dickinson assumed roles and played out dramas for her audiences, including in her poetry. But more than this, she perhaps used the 'persona' of the dramatic monologue to assume male roles, from which society debarred women. There are examples in 327: *'Before I got my eye put out'* and 1072: *'Title divine – is mine!'*

9 Emily Dickinson clearly experienced grave mental anguish, as in the 'terror' of 1861. This is evident when she tries to analyse these experiences in her **'Poems of Definition'**, such as 341: *'After great pain, a formal feeling comes'* and 414: *''Twas like a Maelstrom, with a notch'*.

10 She also struggles to define her system of personal values, evident in poems about **psychological experience**, such as 303: *'The Soul selects her own Society'* and 754: *'My Life had stood – a Loaded Gun'*.

11 It was difficult for a woman in her age to become a full-time 'professional' writer, although Emily Dickinson would not have used that expression. Her writing in a sense forced her to sacrifice social life for poetry, and she frequently explores this in poems about **the problems of writing poetry**, such as 657: *'I dwell in Possibility'* and 1129: *'Tell all the Truth but tell it slant'*.

The Interpretations section of this book (pages 135–186) offers further exploration of literary, philosophical and social/historical contexts. As you become familiar with Emily Dickinson's poetry you will see that a poem may, of course, be placed in more than one context (see Appendix, page 202).

Selected Poems of Emily Dickinson

67 Success is counted sweetest
By those who ne'er succeed.
To comprehend a nectar
Requires sorest need.

5 Not one of all the purple Host
Who took the Flag today
Can tell the definition
So clear of Victory

As he defeated – dying –
10 On whose forbidden ear
The distant strains of triumph
Burst agonized and clear!

79 Going to Heaven!
I don't know when –
Pray do not ask me how!
Indeed I'm too astonished
5 To think of answering you!
Going to Heaven!
How dim it sounds!
And yet it will be done
As sure as flocks go home at night
10 Unto the Shepherd's arm!

Perhaps you're going too!
Who knows?
If you should get there first
Save just a little space for me
15 Close to the two I lost –

The smallest 'Robe' will fit me
And just a bit of 'Crown' –
For you know we do not mind our dress
When we are going home –

20 I'm glad I don't believe it
For it would stop my breath –
And I'd like to look a little more
At such a curious Earth!
I'm glad they did believe it
25 Whom I have never found
Since the mighty Autumn afternoon
I left them in the ground.

199 I'm 'wife'– I've finished that –
That other state –
I'm Czar – I'm 'Woman' now –
It's safer so –

5 How odd the Girl's life looks
Behind this soft Eclipse –
I think that Earth feels so
To folks in Heaven – now –

This being comfort – then –
10 That other kind – was pain –
But why compare?
I'm 'Wife'! Stop there!

211 Come slowly – Eden!
Lips unused to Thee –
Bashful – sip thy Jessamines –
As the fainting Bee –

5 Reaching late his flower,
Round her chamber hums –
Counts his nectars –
Enters – and is lost in Balms.

213 Did the Harebell loose her girdle
To the lover Bee
Would the Bee the Harebell *hallow*
Much as formerly?

5 Did the 'Paradise' – persuaded –
Yield her moat of pearl –
Would the Eden *be* an Eden,
Or the Earl – an *Earl*?

214 I taste a liquor never brewed –
From Tankards scooped in Pearl –
Not all the Vats upon the Rhine
Yield such an Alcohol!

5 Inebriate of Air – am I –
And Debauchee of Dew –
Reeling – thro endless summer days –
From inns of Molten Blue –

When 'Landlords' turn the drunken Bee
10 Out of the Foxglove's door –
When Butterflies – renounce their 'drams' –
I shall but drink the more!

Till Seraphs swing their snowy Hats –
And Saints – to windows run –
15 To see the little Tippler
Leaning against the – Sun –

216 Safe in their Alabaster Chambers –
Untouched by Morning
And untouched by Noon –
Sleep the meek members of the Resurrection –
5 Rafter of satin,
And Roof of stone.

Light laughs the breeze
In her Castle above them –
Babbles the Bee in a stolid Ear,
10 Pipe the Sweet Birds in ignorant cadence –
Ah, what sagacity perished here!

(1859)

Safe in their Alabaster Chambers –
Untouched by Morning –
And untouched by Noon –
Lie the meek members of the Resurrection –
5 Rafter of Satin – and Roof of Stone!

Grand go the Years – in the Crescent – above them –
Worlds scoop their Arcs –
And Firmaments – row –
Diadems – drop – and Doges – surrender –
10 Soundless as dots – on a Disc of Snow –

(1861)

249 Wild Nights – Wild Nights!
Were I with thee
Wild Nights should be
Our luxury!

5 Futile – the Winds –
To a Heart in port –
Done with the Compass –
Done with the Chart!

Rowing in Eden –
10 Ah, the Sea!
Might I but moor – Tonight –
In Thee!

254 'Hope' is the thing with feathers –
That perches in the soul –
And sings the tune without the words –
And never stops – at all –

5 And sweetest – in the Gale – is heard –
And sore must be the storm –
That could abash the little Bird
That kept so many warm –

I've heard it in the chillest land –
10 And on the strangest Sea –
Yet, never, in Extremity,
It asked a crumb – of Me.

258 There's a certain Slant of light,
Winter Afternoons –
That oppresses, like the Heft
Of Cathedral Tunes –

5 Heavenly Hurt, it gives us –
We can find no scar,
But internal difference,
Where the Meanings, are –

None may teach it – Any –
10 'Tis the Seal Despair –
An imperial affliction
Sent us of the Air –

When it comes, the Landscape listens –
Shadows – hold their breath –
15 When it goes, 'tis like the Distance
On the look of Death –

280 I felt a Funeral, in my Brain,
And Mourners to and fro
Kept treading – treading – till it seemed
That Sense was breaking through –

5 And when they all were seated,
A Service, like a Drum –
Kept beating – beating – till I thought
My Mind was going numb –

And then I heard them lift a Box
10 And creak across my Soul
With those same Boots of Lead, again,
Then Space – began to toll,

As all the Heavens were a Bell,
And Being, but an Ear,
15 And I, and Silence, some strange Race
Wrecked, solitary, here –

And then a Plank in Reason, broke,
And I dropped down, and down –
And hit a World, at every plunge,
20 And Finished knowing – then –

288 I'm Nobody! Who are you?
Are you – Nobody – Too?
Then there's a pair of us?
Don't tell! they'd advertise – you know!

5 How dreary – to be – Somebody!
How public – like a Frog –
To tell one's name – the livelong June –
To an admiring Bog!

303 The Soul selects her own Society –
Then – shuts the Door –
To her divine Majority –
Present no more –

5 Unmoved – she notes the Chariots – pausing –
At her low Gate –
Unmoved – an Emperor be kneeling
Upon her Mat –

I've known her – from an ample nation –
10 Choose One –
Then – close the Valves of her attention –
Like Stone –

315 He fumbles at your Soul
As Players at the Keys
Before they drop full Music on –
He stuns you by degrees –
5 Prepares your brittle Nature
For the Ethereal Blow
By fainter Hammers – further heard –
Then nearer – Then so slow
Your Breath has time to straighten –
10 Your Brain – to bubble Cool –
Deals – One – imperial – Thunderbolt –
That scalps your naked Soul –

When Winds take Forests in their Paws –
The Universe – is still –

322 There came a Day at Summer's full,
Entirely for me –
I thought that such were for the Saints,
Where Resurrection – be –

5 The Sun, as common, went abroad,
The flowers, accustomed, blew,
As if no soul the solstice passed
That maketh all things new –

The time was scarce profaned, by speech –
10 The symbol of a word
Was needless, as at Sacrament,
The Wardrobe – of our Lord –

Each was to each The Sealed Church,
Permitted to commune this – time –
15 Lest we too awkward show
At Supper of the Lamb.

The Hours slid fast – as Hours will,
Clutched tight, by greedy hands –
So faces on two Decks, look back,
20 Bound to opposing lands –

And so when all the time had leaked,
Without external sound
Each bound the Other's Crucifix –
We gave no other Bond –

25 Sufficient troth, that we shall rise –
Deposed – at length, the Grave –
To that new Marriage,
Justified – through Calvaries of Love –

327 Before I got my eye put out
I liked as well to see –
As other Creatures, that have Eyes
And know no other way –

5 But were it told to me – Today –
That I might have the sky
For mine – I tell you that my Heart
Would split, for size of me –

The Meadows – mine –
10 The Mountains – mine –
All Forests – Stintless Stars –
As much of Noon as I could take
Between my finite eyes –

The Motions of the Dipping Birds –
15 The Morning's Amber Road –
For mine – to look at when I liked –
The News would strike me dead –

So safer – guess – with just my soul
Upon the Window pane –
20 Where other Creatures put their eyes –
Incautious – of the Sun –

328 A Bird came down the Walk –
He did not know I saw –
He bit an Angleworm in halves
And ate the fellow, raw,

5 And then he drank a Dew
From a convenient Grass –
And then hopped sidewise to the Wall
To let a Beetle pass –

He glanced with rapid eyes
10 That hurried all around –
They looked like frightened Beads, I thought –
He stirred his Velvet Head

Like one in danger, Cautious,
I offered him a Crumb
15 And he unrolled his feathers
And rowed him softer home –

Than Oars divide the Ocean,
Too silver for a seam –
Or Butterflies, off Banks of Noon
20 Leap, plashless as they swim.

341 After great pain, a formal feeling comes –
The Nerves sit ceremonious, like Tombs –
The stiff Heart questions was it He, that bore,
And Yesterday, or Centuries before?

5 The Feet, mechanical, go round –
Of Ground, or Air, or Ought –
A Wooden way
Regardless grown,
A Quartz contentment, like a stone –

10 This is the Hour of Lead –
Remembered, if outlived,
As Freezing persons, recollect the Snow –
First – Chill – then Stupor – then the letting go –

401 What Soft – Cherubic Creatures –
These Gentlewomen are –
One would as soon assault a Plush –
Or violate a Star –

5 Such Dimity Convictions –
A Horror so refined
Of freckled Human Nature –
Of Deity – ashamed –

It's such a common – Glory –
10 A Fisherman's – Degree –
Redemption – Brittle Lady –
Be so – ashamed of Thee –

414 'Twas like a Maelstrom, with a notch,
That nearer, every Day,
Kept narrowing its boiling Wheel
Until the Agony

5 Toyed coolly with the final inch
Of your delirious Hem –
And you dropt, lost,
When something broke –
And let you from a Dream –

10 As if a Goblin with a Gauge –
Kept measuring the Hours –
Until you felt your Second
Weigh, helpless, in his Paws –

And not a Sinew – stirred – could help,
15 And sense was setting numb –
When God – remembered – and the Fiend
Let go, then, Overcome –

As if your Sentence stood – pronounced –
And you were frozen led
20 From Dungeon's luxury of Doubt
To Gibbets, and the Dead –

And when the Film had stitched your eyes
A Creature gasped 'Reprieve'!
Which Anguish was the utterest – then –
25 To perish, or to live?

441 This is my letter to the World
That never wrote to Me –
The simple News that Nature told –
With tender Majesty

5 Her Message is committed
To Hands I cannot see –
For love of Her – Sweet – countrymen –
Judge tenderly – of Me

444 It feels a shame to be Alive –
When Men so brave – are dead –
One envies the Distinguished Dust –
Permitted – such a Head –

5 The Stone – that tells defending Whom
This Spartan put away
What little of Him we – possessed
In Pawn for Liberty –

The price is great – Sublimely paid –
10 Do we deserve – a Thing –
That lives – like Dollars – must be piled
Before we may obtain?

Are we that wait – sufficient worth –
That such Enormous Pearl
15 As life – dissolved be – for Us –
In Battle's – horrid Bowl?

It may be – a Renown to live –
I think the Man who die –
Those unsustained – Saviors –
20 Present Divinity –

446 I showed her Heights she never saw –
'Would'st Climb,' I said?
She said – 'Not so' –
'With *me* –' I said – With *me*?
5 I showed her Secrets – Morning's Nest –
The Rope the Nights were put across –
And *now* – 'Would'st have me for a Guest?'
She could not find her Yes –
And then, I brake my life – And Lo,
10 A Light, for her, did solemn glow,
The larger, as her face withdrew –
And *could* she, further, 'No'?

465 I heard a Fly buzz – when I died –
The Stillness in the Room
Was like the Stillness in the Air –
Between the Heaves of Storm –

5 The Eyes around – had wrung them dry –
And Breaths were gathering firm
For that last Onset – when the King
Be witnessed – in the Room –

I willed my Keepsakes – Signed away
10 What portion of me be
Assignable – and then it was
There interposed a Fly –

With Blue – uncertain stumbling Buzz –
Between the light – and me –
15 And then the Windows failed – and then
I could not see to see –

501 This World is not Conclusion.
A Species stands beyond –
Invisible, as Music –
But positive, as Sound –
5 It beckons, and it baffles –
Philosophy – don't know –
And through a Riddle, at the last –
Sagacity, must go –
To guess it, puzzles scholars –
10 To gain it, Men have borne
Contempt of Generations
And Crucifixion, shown –
Faith slips – and laughs, and rallies –
Blushes, if any see –
15 Plucks at a twig of Evidence –
And asks a Vane, the way –
Much Gesture, from the Pulpit –
Strong Hallelujahs roll –
Narcotics cannot still the Tooth
20 That nibbles at the soul –

510 It was not Death, for I stood up,
And all the Dead, lie down –
It was not Night, for all the Bells
Put out their Tongues, for Noon.

5 It was not Frost, for on my Flesh
I felt Siroccos – crawl –
Nor Fire – for just my Marble feet
Could keep a Chancel, cool –

And yet, it tasted, like them all,
10 The Figures I have seen
Set orderly, for Burial,
Reminded me, of mine –

As if my life were shaven,
And fitted to a frame,
15 And could not breathe without a key,
And 'twas like Midnight, some –

When everything that ticked – has stopped –
And Space stares all around –
Or Grisly frosts – first Autumn morns,
20 Repeal the Beating Ground –

But, most, like Chaos – Stopless – cool –
Without a Chance, or Spar –
Or even a Report of Land –
To justify – Despair.

512 The Soul has Bandaged moments –
When too appalled to stir –
She feels some ghastly Fright come up
And stop to look at her –

5 Salute her – with long fingers –
Caress her freezing hair –
Sip, Goblin, from the very lips
The Lover – hovered – o'er –
Unworthy, that a thought so mean
10 Accost a Theme – so – fair –

The soul has moments of Escape –
When bursting all the doors –
She dances like a Bomb, abroad,
And swings upon the Hours,

15 As do the Bee – delirious borne –
Long Dungeoned from his Rose –
Touch Liberty – then know no more,
But Noon, and Paradise –

The Soul's retaken moments –
20 When, Felon led along,
With shackles on the plumed feet,
And staples, in the Song,

The Horror welcomes her, again,
These, are not brayed of Tongue –

528 Mine – by the Right of the White Election!
Mine – by the Royal Seal!
Mine – by the Sign in the Scarlet prison –
Bars – cannot conceal!

5 Mine – here – in Vision – and in Veto!
Mine – by the Grave's Repeal –
Titled – Confirmed –
Delirious Charter!
Mine – long as Ages steal!

585 I like to see it lap the Miles –
And lick the Valleys up –
And stop to feed itself at Tanks –
And then – prodigious step

5 Around a Pile of Mountains –
And supercilious peer
In Shanties – by the sides of Roads –
And then a Quarry pare

To fit its Ribs
10 And crawl between
Complaining all the while
In horrid – hooting stanza –
Then chase itself down Hill –

And neigh like Boanerges –
15 Then – punctual as a Star
Stop – docile and omnipotent
At its own stable door –

640 I cannot live with You –
It would be Life –
And Life is over there –
Behind the Shelf

5 The Sexton keeps the Key to –
Putting up
Our Life – His Porcelain –
Like a Cup –

Discarded of the Housewife –
10 Quaint – or Broke –
A newer Sevres pleases –
Old Ones crack –

I could not die – with You –
For One must wait
15 To shut the Other's Gaze down –
You – could not –

And I – Could I stand by
And see You – freeze –
Without my Right of Frost –
20 Death's privilege?

Nor could I rise – with You –
Because Your Face
Would put out Jesus' –
That New Grace

25 Glow plain – and foreign
On my homesick Eye –
Except that You than He
Shone closer by –

They'd judge Us – How –
30 For You – served Heaven – You know,
Or sought to –
I could not –

Because You saturated Sight –
And I had no more Eyes,
35 For sordid excellence
As Paradise

And were You lost, I would be –
Though My Name
Rang loudest
40 On the Heavenly fame –

And were You – saved –
And I – condemned to be
Where You were not –
That self – were Hell to Me –

45 So We must meet apart –
You there – I – here –
With just the Door ajar
That Oceans are – and Prayer –
And that White Sustenance –
50 Despair –

657 I dwell in Possibility –
A fairer House than Prose –
More numerous of Windows –
Superior – for Doors –

5 Of Chambers as the Cedars –
Impregnable of Eye –
And for an Everlasting Roof
The Gambrels of the Sky –

Of Visions – the fairest –
10 For Occupation – This –
The spreading wide my narrow Hands
To gather Paradise –

663 Again – his voice is at the door –
I feel the old *Degree* –
I hear him ask the servant
For such an one – as me –

5 I take a *flower* – as I go –
My face to *justify* –
He never *saw* me – *in this life* –
I might *surprise* his eye!

I cross the Hall with *mingled* steps –
10 I – silent – pass the door –
I look on all this world *contains* –
Just his face – nothing more!

We talk in *careless* – and in *toss* –
A kind of *plummet* strain
15 Each – sounding – shyly –
Just – how – deep –
The *other's* one – had been –

We *walk* – I leave my Dog – at home –
A *tender* – *thoughtful* Moon
20 Goes with us – just a little way –
And – then – we are *alone* –

Alone – if *Angels* are 'alone' –
First time they *try* the *sky*!
Alone – if those 'veiled faces' – be –
25 We cannot *count* – on High!

I'd give – to live that hour – *again* –
The *purple* – *in my Vein* –
But *He* must *count the drops* – *himself* –
My *price* for *every stain*!

668 'Nature' is what we see –
The Hill – the Afternoon –
Squirrel – Eclipse – the Bumble bee –
Nay – Nature is Heaven –
5 Nature is what we hear –
The Bobolink – the Sea –
Thunder – the Cricket –
Nay – Nature is Harmony –
Nature is what we know –
10 Yet have no art to say –
So impotent Our Wisdom is
To her Simplicity.

670 One need not be a Chamber – to be Haunted –
One need not be a House –
The Brain has Corridors – surpassing
Material Place –

5 Far safer, of a Midnight Meeting
External Ghost
Than its interior Confronting –
That Cooler Host.

Far safer, through an Abbey gallop,
10 The Stones a'chase –
Than Unarmed, one's a'self encounter –
In lonesome Place –

Ourself behind ourself, concealed –
Should startle most –
15 Assassin hid in our Apartment
Be Horror's least.

The Body – borrows a Revolver –
He bolts the Door –
O'erlooking a superior spectre –
20 Or More –

690 Victory comes late –
And is held low to freezing lips –
Too rapt with frost
To take it –
5 How sweet it would have tasted –
Just a Drop –
Was God so economical?
His Table's spread too high for Us –
Unless We dine on tiptoe –
10 Crumbs – fit such little mouths –
Cherries – suit Robins –
The Eagle's Golden Breakfast strangles – Them –
God keep His Oath to Sparrows –
Who of little Love – know how to starve –

709 Publication – is the Auction
Of the Mind of Man –
Poverty – be justifying
For so foul a thing

5 Possibly – but We – would rather
From Our Garret go
White – Unto the White Creator –
Than invest – Our Snow –

Thought belong to Him who gave it –
10 Then – to Him Who bear
Its Corporeal illustration – Sell
The Royal Air –

In the Parcel – Be the Merchant
Of the Heavenly Grace –
15 But reduce no Human Spirit
To Disgrace of Price –

712 Because I could not stop for Death –
He kindly stopped for me –
The Carriage held but just Ourselves –
And Immortality.

5 We slowly drove – He knew no haste
And I had put away
My labor and my leisure too,
For His Civility –

We passed the School, where Children strove
10 At Recess – in the Ring –
We passed the Fields of Gazing Grain –
We passed the Setting Sun –

Or rather – He passed Us –
The Dews drew quivering and chill –
15 For only Gossamer, my Gown –
My Tippet – only Tulle –

We paused before a House that seemed
A Swelling of the Ground –
The Roof was scarcely visible –
20 The Cornice – in the Ground –

Since then – 'tis Centuries – and yet
Feels shorter than the Day
I first surmised the Horses' Heads
Were toward Eternity –

732 She rose to His Requirement – dropt
The Playthings of Her Life
To take the honorable Work
Of Woman, and of Wife –

5 If ought She missed in Her new Day,
Of Amplitude, or Awe –
Or first Prospective – Or the Gold
In using, wear away,

It lay unmentioned – as the Sea
10 Develops Pearl, and Weed,
But only to Himself – be known
The Fathoms they abide –

741 Drama's Vitallest Expression is the Common Day
That arise and set about Us –
Other Tragedy

Perish in the Recitation –
5 This – the best enact
When the Audience is scattered
And the Boxes shut –

'Hamlet' to Himself were Hamlet –
Had not Shakespeare wrote –
10 Though the 'Romeo' left no Record
Of his Juliet,

It were infinite enacted
In the Human Heart –
Only Theatre recorded
15 Owner cannot shut –

747 It dropped so low – in my Regard –
I heard it hit the Ground –
And go to pieces on the Stones
At bottom of my Mind –

5 Yet blamed the Fate that flung it – less
Than I denounced Myself,
For entertaining Plated Wares
Upon my Silver Shelf –

754 My Life had stood – a Loaded Gun –
In Corners – till a Day
The Owner passed – identified –
And carried Me away –

5 And now We roam in Sovereign Woods –
And now We hunt the Doe –
And every time I speak for Him –
The Mountains straight reply –

And do I smile, such cordial light
10 Upon the Valley glow –
It is as a Vesuvian face
Had let its pleasure through –

And when at Night – Our good Day done –
I guard My Master's Head –
15 'Tis better than the Eider-Duck's
Deep Pillow – to have shared –

To foe of His – I'm deadly foe –
None stir the second time –
On whom I lay a Yellow Eye –
20 Or an emphatic Thumb –

Though I than He – may longer live
He longer must – than I –
For I have but the power to kill,
Without – the power to die –

986 A narrow Fellow in the Grass
Occasionally rides –
You may have met Him – did you not
His notice sudden is –

5 The Grass divides as with a Comb –
A spotted shaft is seen –
And then it closes at your feet
And opens further on –

He likes a Boggy Acre
10 A Floor too cool for Corn –
Yet when a Boy, and Barefoot –
I more than once at Noon
Have passed, I thought, a Whip lash
Unbraiding in the Sun
15 When stooping to secure it
It wrinkled, and was gone –

Several of Nature's People
I know, and they know me –
I feel for them a transport
20 Of cordiality –

But never met this Fellow
Attended, or alone
Without a tighter breathing
And Zero at the Bone –

1068 Further in Summer than the Birds
Pathetic from the Grass
A minor Nation celebrates
Its unobtrusive Mass.

5 No Ordinance be seen
So gradual the Grace
A pensive Custom it becomes
Enlarging Loneliness.

Antiquest felt at Noon
10 When August burning low
Arise this spectral Canticle
Repose to typify

Remit as yet no Grace
No Furrow on the Glow
15 Yet a Druidic Difference
Enhances Nature now

1072 Title divine – is mine!
The Wife – without the Sign!
Acute Degree – conferred on me –
Empress of Calvary!
5 Royal – all but the Crown!
Betrothed – without the swoon
God sends us Women –
When you – hold – Garnet to Garnet –
Gold – to Gold –
10 Born – Bridalled – Shrouded –
In a Day –
Tri Victory
'My Husband' – women say –
Stroking the Melody –
15 Is *this* – the way?

1100 The last Night that She lived
It was a Common Night
Except the Dying – this to Us
Made Nature different

5 We noticed smallest things –
Things overlooked before
By this great light upon our Minds
Italicized – as 'twere.

As We went out and in
10 Between Her final Room
And Rooms where Those to be alive
Tomorrow were, a Blame

That Others could exist
While She must finish quite
15 A Jealousy for Her arose
So nearly infinite –

We waited while She passed –
It was a narrow time –
Too jostled were Our Souls to speak
20 At length the notice came.

She mentioned, and forgot –
Then lightly as a Reed
Bent to the Water, struggled scarce –
Consented, and was dead –

25 And We – We placed the Hair –
And drew the Head erect –
And then an awful leisure was
Belief to regulate –

1129 Tell all the Truth but tell it slant –
Success in Circuit lies
Too bright for our infirm Delight
The Truth's superb surprise

5 As Lightning to the Children eased
With explanation kind
The Truth must dazzle gradually
Or every man be blind –

1138 A Spider sewed at Night
Without a Light
Upon an Arc of White.

If Ruff it was of Dame
5 Or Shroud of Gnome
Himself himself inform.

Of Immortality
His Strategy
Was Physiognomy.

1183 Step lightly on this narrow spot –
The broadest Land that grows
Is not so ample as the Breast
These Emerald Seams enclose.

5 Step lofty, for this name be told
As far as Cannon dwell
Or Flag subsist or Fame export
Her deathless Syllable.

1263 There is no Frigate like a Book
To take us Lands away
Nor any Coursers like a Page
Of prancing Poetry –
5 This Traverse may the poorest take
Without oppress of Toll –
How frugal is the Chariot
That bears the Human soul.

1286 I thought that nature was enough
Till Human nature came
But that the other did absorb
As Parallax a Flame –

5 Of Human nature just aware
There added the Divine
Brief struggle for capacity
The power to contain

Is always as the contents
10 But give a Giant room
And you will lodge a Giant
And not a smaller man

1551 Those – dying then,
Knew where they went –
They went to God's Right Hand –
That Hand is amputated now
5 And God cannot be found –

The abdication of Belief
Makes the Behavior small –
Better an ignis fatuus
Than no illume at all –

1670 In Winter in my Room
I came upon a Worm –
Pink, lank and warm –
But as he was a worm
5 And worms presume
Not quite with him at home –
Secured him by a string
To something neighboring
And went along.

10 A Trifle afterward
A thing occurred
I'd not believe it if I heard
But state with creeping blood –
A snake with mottles rare
15 Surveyed my chamber floor
In feature as the worm before
But ringed with power –

The very string with which
I tied him – too
20 When he was mean and new
That string was there –

I shrank – 'How fair you are'!
Propitiation's claw –
'Afraid,' he hissed
25 'Of me'?
'No cordiality' –

He fathomed me –
Then to a Rhythm *Slim*
Secreted in his Form
30 As Patterns swim
Projected him.

That time I flew
Both eyes his way
Lest he pursue
35 Nor ever ceased to run
Till in a distant Town
Towns on from mine
I set me down
This was a dream.

Notes

Technical terms used in these notes are defined in the Glossary, pages 196–201.

67 Success is counted sweetest

In this lyric poem Emily Dickinson presents one of her central concerns: the futility of war. There is no shrillness and no excessive emotion; instead she presents a quiet, carefully developed (although compressed) argument. The poem suggests the argument is unanswerable, and the poem therefore has an epigrammatic tone. Dickinson's language is shot through with irony, as this war poem suggests that the true meaning of victory may only be realized by the defeated. In a more general sense, it could also be true that those things we most want are the things we cannot have.

This poem is typical of Dickinson's war poetry in that it is not about a specific battle, or even tied by specific references to any precise time period. Instead she develops her ideas along universal principles of loss/gain, justice/injustice, pain and suffering. For this reason her poetry does not date.

The quiet tone is created by the alliteration on 's' and the fairly regular rhythm and rhyme scheme. In the first two stanzas there is a mixture of full rhyme (*succeed/need*, 2/4) and half-rhyme (*today/Victory*, 6/8), and in line 5 there is an extra syllable; perhaps together these devices suggest the length of the exhausting struggle or the weariness of the battle. From line 4 the struggle and the battle seem to be lost on both levels; there is no victory nor any hope of life. In the last stanza, the poet seems confident of proving her point in the final three lines, as the regular rhythm reappears, the poem ends abruptly with full masculine rhyme, *ear/clear* (10/12), and there is a final exclamation mark, almost like a shout of anger. It is an explosive and angered ending to a quiet poem, as if the poet is saying that no one could possibly contradict her.

In poems like this, although it is a lyric poem, Dickinson keeps the 'I' persona out of the poem to give the effect of detachment. A contrast is drawn between the victors and the defeated. Is there any sign of optimism here? Perhaps Dickinson sees victory or success as better than defeat; or perhaps it is the reverse. On the other hand we could be faced with two negatives about the outcome of war. War would appear to be absolutely futile as no one really gains. There appears to be no suggestion of a religious belief that suffering will be rewarded in heaven.

The poem ends on a note of paradox, as do so many of Dickinson's poems; success might be counted as sweetest, but only by those who cannot grasp it because they are dying. The victors will never feel this, so what is the point of victory, therefore what is the point of war? Paradoxes arise because Dickinson works so often by establishing opposites that can seldom be reconciled.

1–2 These lines define the proposition of the poem: success is more valued by the defeated than by the victors.

1 The poem begins with the use of alliteration on soft 's' sounds; this might suggest a tone of quiet confidence.

3–4 Here the reader is told who can and who cannot understand success.

2/4 The full rhyme of *succeed* and *need*, as with the full rhyme of 10/12, might perhaps be used to create a sense of certainty on the author's part, as if the poem is offering an aphorism.

3 **nectar** the fluid bees sip from flowers, and the name given to the drink of the gods. There is a typical use of metaphor here in the word 'nectar'; whenever Dickinson creates an abstract argument she uses very concrete – and in this case sensory – images to illustrate her points. There is some irony in relating the drink of the gods to war.

4 The alliteration on 's' is replaced by that on 't', so the quiet tone is continued.

6 Dickinson refers to the whole army as the *Flag*: this is a metonym and is another typical device of her poetry, which creates compression, and offers a clear visual image.

6/8 The half-rhymes of *today* and *Victory* replace the full rhyme of the first and third stanzas, perhaps to avoid a break in the line of thought.

8–9 These lines link the stanzas by enjambment to present a complete thought developed by the end of the poem.

9 The quiet 's' and the 't' alliteration of the first and second stanzas is replaced by the thudding 'd' of the last stanza – as in the second version of 216: '*Safe in their Alabaster Chambers*'. This might suggest both the weariness of the defeated army trudging along, and also the tolling of a funeral bell.

79 Going to Heaven!

The persona in this apparently playful poem assumes the voice of a young child of unknown gender. The scenario suggested is that he or she has perhaps been to a funeral, and been told by an adult that dead friends have 'gone to heaven'. The persona continues to develop her thoughts in this dramatic monologue in an initially naïve tone, beginning by thinking about heaven; a contrast is created between life in heaven and life on earth. In a child-like way, the speaker imagines the miniature clothes that would dress her like a saint. It is as if she plays with the idea of going to heaven.

Suddenly there is a change at line 20. The tone is of a child suddenly growing up, or might it be that the mask of the persona is dropped for a while? The idea of heaven seems to become shocking: or is it the idea of leaving this lively earth? In the last stanza a further clear contrast is established between *I/we* and *they* (19–24): non-believers and believers. This speaker will hear no suggestions of life after death in a mysterious place called heaven.

Each of the three stanzas follows the three stages of the speaker's argument as he or she moves from joy at the thought of heaven to playful, child-like comments about going to heaven herself, and finally an equally vivid rejection of heaven in favour of life on earth.

This is typical of Dickinson's poems about death and immortality; she is an existentialist in that she seems to believe that our experiences on earth count for so much to us, especially when promises of redemption, salvation and resurrection can never be proved. As is typical of Dickinson's poetry, her own views are separate from the views of the naïve young speaker of the poem; this allows for the irony of a dramatic monologue as the poet and the reader know much more than the speaker, who is seen to be working through his or her ideas as the poem progresses. As a speaker intervenes between the poet and the reader, Dickinson's private views cannot be known. Another typical aspect of this poem is that Dickinson presents apparently conventional views, only to undermine them as the poem develops, and further increase the ironies of the poem, as she does in 216: '*Safe in their Alabaster Chambers*'.

1–10 The many exclamation marks of the first stanza capture the excited imagination of the speaker.

7 To the speaker, heaven sounds *dim* and beyond her imagination.

15 As the tone changes, so does the punctuation of the second stanza, as the dashes suggest that the speaker has paused to think about what he or she is saying.

16–18 Because heaven sounds so far away, the speaker tries to relate it to his or her home life in the domestic images of clothing in stanza 2, with the '*Robe*', and *dress* for *going home*.

19–20 A sudden change of tone, with the hard consonants of 'g' and 'd'; there is the shock rejection of the idea of heaven.

20–27 There is little punctuation as the tone becomes more assertive.

22 The alliterative chiming of *I'd like to look a little more* re-establishes the naïve tone.

23–26 In the last stanza the speaker's thoughts turn to this life on earth. *Earth* is *curious*, and nature is *mighty*, whereas heaven is *dim*; obviously life on earth has more appeal for the speaker.

24 The poet presents a contrast between the *we* of line 19 and *they* who are believers in line 24. There is no doubt that the speaker is sceptical of ideas of resurrection and heaven.

199 I'm 'wife' – I've finished that

This poem is about the effects of marriage upon women, and is one of the poems in which there is a clear enquiry about personal identity. The female persona of this dramatic monologue is a (newly?) married woman looking back at her girlhood life, comparing it to her present status as *'wife'*. She appears to be searching for a new identity. The word *that* in the first line is intriguing: to what does it refer? In the course of the poem the reader realizes that the reference is to girlhood. But the idea is not developed. The speaker won't allow herself to reflect on her former life. It would seem that marriage both empowers (*Czar*) and overshadows the woman (*Eclipse*). The crucial question of whether marriage is happier for a woman than girlhood is not considered; the speaker abruptly refuses even to remember her youthful past. The reason for this is unclear, but the reader perhaps infers that the woman cannot allow herself such thoughts. In a way, the omission is much more significant than words.

Is there finally any sense of a positive gain in marriage for a woman? The role of the wife initially seems to be presented conventionally, in a way that society would approve, but the overall meaning and mood of the poem ironically undermine this. Perhaps there is a suggestion that the woman may suffer the fate of many women in the nineteenth century in being forced into a role of passivity, acceptance and powerlessness – one that Dickinson herself could not tolerate. Again, this poem rests on a conflict, this time between being a wife and girlhood.

Dickinson very much admired Robert Browning's poetry, including his dramatic monologues; she adapted this form for herself by making superficially conventional views work ironically. The words of the persona of this poem seem to undermine her claims for her new status. In Dickinson's poetry each persona exists in only one particular poem; the speaker creates her own identity, and then is usually seen to ironically undermine her own claims, implicitly or explicitly. Dramatic irony arises as the reader becomes more aware of the true situation than the speaker. For these reasons, this poem is a good model to use for discussion of Dickinson's dramatic monologues.

1 The opening of the poem is typically striking: is the complex tone excited? Or puzzled? Or proud? What is the *that* which is *finished*? The reader's curiosity is aroused. The use of inverted commas draws the reader's attention to the subject matter of the poem. The use of dashes here and throughout the poem suggests ongoing thought, up to the question in 11 and the abrupt exclamation mark of the last line.

3 **Czar** a powerful Emperor of Russia up to time of the revolution. Dickinson uses the power-related word to define the married woman's status at first; but there is a contradiction in the next stanza.

6 An *Eclipse* occurs when one astronomical body obscures the light of another, wholly or partially. This metaphor contradicts the idea of the *Czar*. The word *soft* implies something so gentle that it is barely noticeable. Perhaps marriage both empowers and casts into shadow. Perhaps Dickinson is criticizing the propaganda of a male-dominated society.

9 The word *comfort*, along with *safer* (4) and *soft* (6), conveys security rather than excitement or joy.

12 Dickinson sets up a contrast between girlhood and '*Wife*', but does not follow this through. The strong final imperative verb *Stop there!* may be addressed to the speaker, to the poet herself, or to the reader. Perhaps it is felt to be unwise to carry further the contrast which the poem had started to establish between girl and wife. The impact of the two final lines with their full rhyme creates a sudden and abrupt change of tone to end the poem, perhaps indecisively.

211 Come slowly – Eden!

This is a poem about desiring someone or something and the effects of achieving this desire. Dickinson uses the sensuous and sensual image of the bee and the flower to express an abstract idea, and the poem seems to have a general and also a more specific sexual connotation. The presumably female speaker of this dramatic monologue speaks of achieving something long desired, but also of the dangers of being overcome by sudden and unaccustomed joy. On one level, there may be an indirect warning to both men and women here about social attitudes to sex, marriage or society, as in 199: '*I'm "wife" – I've finished that*'. In this sense the poet offers considerations about conventional female identity, and about male identity. After consummation, the bee is *lost*; might there be social parallels for both men and women here? What might happen to a woman once male desire has been satisfied? How might a man behave if he is considered to be *lost*? Perhaps the reduction of the speaker to a pair of lips, an ambiguous sexual image, is a warning to both men and women about the dangers of too much and too sudden satisfaction of a desire. However, there is also a more general meaning about the dangers of wanting something so badly that achieving it causes serious damage. In this case it is possible to see the lips as a gateway to any physical desire, or as a reminder that there is a speaker who is offering a moral fable.

Again the poem is structured on a contrast: before and after the desired thing/person is gained. Religious language used to support secular ideas is particularly evident in 322: '*There came a Day at Summer's full*'. Perhaps the word *Eden* here stresses the intensity of the desire and of the pleasure in achieving this desire.

1 The first line announces the theme of the poem directly. The dash before the word *Eden* declares the significance of this word, supported by the exclamation mark. The use of dashes throughout the poem creates the sense of an ongoing, irresistible movement as the speaker develops her thoughts.

2 Here the speaker is reduced to a pair of lips using synecdoche; there is similar usage in 280: '*I felt a Funeral, in my Brain*' (in this case, an ear), and in 327: '*Before I got my eye put out*', where the speaker is reduced to a *soul*. This is an emblematic and visual reminder to the reader of what this poem is about.

2–4 The register, such as *lips* and *Bashful*, and the delicate example of the bee entering the flower, may suggest that the speaker is a sensitive female.

3–8 Words such as *sip*, *fainting* and *lost* convey the sensuous and sensual experience underlined by the word *Enters*, which has sexual connotations. The ideas are linked by dashes creating enjambment, which gives the sense of an ongoing thought and also perhaps of entrapment.

3 **Jessamines** jasmines, fragrant flowers.

4 Introduces the simile of the bee, which is sustained throughout the poem.

5–8 The image of the bee entering the flower represents in general the achievement of a desire, but in specific terms may have sexual connotations.

8 **Balms** soothing lotions. The word *lost* raises a doubt about the wisdom of achieving such an experience. It is typical of Dickinson that sexual experience is conveyed by a natural image, as in 249: '*Wild Nights – Wild Nights!*' and 1072: '*Title divine – is mine!*'.

213 Did the Harebell loose her girdle

This poem, like 211: '*Come slowly – Eden!*', is about achieving something once desired, although the precise focus differs slightly and the image is rather more playful. Here the writer offers a discussion about whether something will hold as much value after it has been achieved as before. On one level, this is a poem about achieving something long desired; however, this poem might relate to the roles and attitudes of males. There might also be suggestions about female roles and attitudes, which may be seen as a warning to women. Perhaps, because of the use of the image of the *girdle* (1), this poem relates more explicitly to women than poem 211. How much value will they continue to hold in the man's eyes after sexual consummation? It might be a warning to women about valuing their identity and selfhood rather than yielding to the persuasion of men in both sexual and general terms. By extending the imagery of the poem to include *Paradise* (5), perhaps Dickinson opens up the meanings of the poem to include all objects of desire for both men and women, linking this poem to 732: '*She rose to His Requirement – dropt*'. The poem may be seen as a rather playful moral fable.

Another level of meaning is attached if the word *Earl* (8) is seen as a pun. One of Dickinson's fellow female writers was called Eliza Earle; she also believed that writing poetry gave women some power in society. So this pun might further develop the meanings of the poem.

Again there is a conflict between two perspectives – before and after a consummation. Again religious imagery and language are used to explain a secular experience, in *Paradise* (5) and *pearl* (6); what might these usages suggest about Dickinson's attitude to life on earth and the idea of immortality?

The full rhymes of both stanzas combine with the strong and regular rhythm to make this a musical and light-hearted poem.

1 The word *Did* is in the subjunctive mood, to indicate that this is a speculative proposition. The opening image of the harebell loosing her girdle to the bee has sexual connotations, specifically in the word *girdle*. Typically, Dickinson uses natural imagery, as in 211: '*Come slowly – Eden!*', to develop a sexual theme. Perhaps this 'filtering' effect removes suggestions of overt sexuality from the poem.

3–8 The words *hallow*, *be* and *earl* are italicized to stress the question that is being asked.

5–8 The use of dashes drives home the meanings in the second stanza by suggesting that the speaker is slowly and carefully picking her words.

214 I taste a liquor never brewed

In this poem Dickinson toys with the idea of drunkenness, and being drunk on the joys of life. She playfully describes a person going from inn to inn until the sun goes down; even the inhabitants of heaven, angels and saints, are drawn to the energy and joy of the *little Tippler* (15). These joys suggest that the pleasures of life are preferable to those of heaven, as in 79: '*Going to Heaven!*'; even the angels and saints feel compelled to take part. This is a typical motif in Dickinson's poetry. It might suggest that the writer, as in poem 79, would prefer the joys of life on earth rather than trust in resurrection and the joys of heaven. Or perhaps the *little Tippler* who is *Leaning against the Sun* (15–16) is already immortal, and has achieved a 'heaven' which is a continuation of the joys of life on earth.

As usual Dickinson draws on several registers to achieve effects here. The language of the temperance movement is playfully turned on its head; there are the natural images of the *Foxglove's* inn (10), and the drunken bee, which might serve to take away any negative social connotations of drunkenness, because it is portrayed as natural; then there is religious language drawing in the saints and angels at the end of the poem.

This poem reflects a social context of the poet's time, the powerful temperance movement, which exhorted people to give up alcohol for the sake of their souls and for the good of society. This is the language that Dickinson playfully picks up and turns on its head; it is worth thinking about what this might suggest about her response to this social context.

This musical poem is written in common metre, the rhythm of English hymns. This is appropriate in that the poem becomes a hymn to the pleasures of life on earth. The poem rests on one central image of being drunk, supported by a register related to drinking such as *Alcohol* (4), *Inebriate* (5), and *Debauchee* (6), playfully sustained throughout the whole poem.

The increasing use of dashes and enjambment throughout the poem creates a fast pace, so that this poem buzzes and fizzes with energy.

2/4 The half-rhyme of *Pearl* and *Alcohol* helps to maintain the speed and sense of continuity of the poem without end stopping.

5 **Inebriate** drunk.

7 The active verb *Reeling* at the start of the line contrasts well with the word *Leaning* (16), which draws the poem and the energetic exercise to a peaceful conclusion.

9–11 Again, as in 211: *'Come slowly – Eden!'* and 213: *'Did the Harebell loose her girdle'*, natural imagery is used to filter the ideas and get rid of unpleasant connotations. The comic references, with a flower for insects in place of a pub, keep the playful tone to support the idea of the speaker being drunk on the joys of life.

11 **dram** a measure of alcohol, especially Scotch whisky.

13–14 Even the saints are attracted to the fun and run to look, swinging their white hats. There could be a hidden reference to a popular American tune of swing and jazz music, *When the saints go marching in.*

15 The word *little* seems endearing.

16 The register moves away from nature and towards that of heaven and eternity. The tone becomes a little more solemn. The word *Sun* carries a religious pun on the 'son of God'; the word *Leaning* combined with the word *Sun* conveys a sense of life ending as the sun sets.

216 Safe in their Alabaster Chambers

There are two versions of this poem; Dickinson sent the original version to her friend Sue Gilbert for review, and the second version was written after her comments were received. The speaker looks at a carved tomb or sepulchre and reflects on the people buried there, and begins to wonder about death, resurrection and immortality.

1859 version

Dickinson again presents her ideas through a series of oppositions; there is a contrast between the first stanza and the second; between the dead and the living; and wordplay on darkness and light.

The first stanza seems to offer a hopeful image of resurrection, but after reading the words *Safe* (1) and *meek* (4), this may be interpreted ironically. The dead were obviously wealthy with their satin-lined coffins, so perhaps it is assumed that they will be among the 'Elect', sure of resurrection. However, the *Roof of stone* (6) could be seen, along with the soft satin, as suggesting entrapment, as the dead are seen to be deprived of light and life in the second stanza.

In the second stanza the dead are contrasted with images of light and life as the natural cycle of life goes on. There seems little hope in this poem for resurrection after death.

The poem also implies a scathing attack on the materialism of certain Puritans who smugly linked financial and social success with the certainty of going to heaven. The subjects of the poem have spent money on their tomb, but they cannot buy their way to salvation. The poem's response to beliefs in resurrection would have shocked some of the contemporary audience.

These poems show the use of three of Dickinson's central devices:

- the setting up of oppositions without reconciling the differences (the dead contrasted first with natural life [1859] and then with time and space [1861])
- the uses of dashes to vary the rhythm of the poetry and to create other effects
- the inclusion of registers from different contexts within a poem: here there are registers of nature (1859) and religion, history and astronomy (1861).

1 **Alabaster** a pure white stone from which statues are carved; this suggests that the tomb was expensive, so the dead were once rich. The dead might seem *Safe* in their grand tomb, but perhaps there is an irony as maybe the dead are also safe from resurrection?

2–3 The repetition of the word *Untouched*, heavily stressed at the beginning of the second line, reminds the reader that the dead are quite remote from any changes on earth.

4 **members of the Resurrection** Christians believing in salvation and heaven; perhaps *meek* suggests complacency about this and is therefore also ironical. This long line might suggest a very long *Sleep*.

5 The *Rafter of satin* suggests an expensive coffin lined with satin.

6 The *Roof of stone*, weighty words for the roof of the tomb, suggests that it would be impossible to get out.

7–11 The second stanza, in contrast, concentrates on life rather than death. There is the alliteration on *Lightly laughs*, *Babbles the Bee* (9) and *Sweet Birds* (10) to stress bright and happy images of movement and vitality.

10 The birds are said to be *ignorant*, but they live in happy harmony. Could this be another ironical comment on the validity of religious belief?

11 The word *sagacity*, which means wisdom, supports the ironical tone, as does the word *perished*; there is absolutely no hint of life after death. The fact that the second stanza is cut off one line shorter than the first also suggests the suddenness and completeness of death.

1861 version

Dickinson changed the second stanza considerably. Instead of a contrast using nature, the poet uses the larger scale of history, time and space. Perhaps this makes the sense of loss in death even greater, or it might make human life appear extremely insignificant set against universal frames. Dickinson might be presenting some of her own doubts about resurrection in these two poems, but she may also be criticizing Puritan doctrines and practices. The word *Sleep* of the first version, which may well suggest a possible awakening, perhaps in heaven, has become the inert and lifeless *Lie* in the second version.

5 Dickinson has run together lines 5 and 6 of the first version. What is the effect of this?

6–10 The increased use of dashes in the second stanza may add to the feeling of weight and deadness; Dickinson uses touch, sight and sound effectively in this stanza.

9 **Doges** rulers of Venice several hundred years ago. They, too, have disappeared. Again there is a sense of the brevity and insignificance of human life, even for the wealthy and powerful.

9–10 There are different uses of alliteration in this version: note especially the repeated use of the letter 'd', which may imply deadness and the sound of funeral bells.

10 The idea of whiteness is repeated at the end of the poem: everything seems to disappear from our view, just as human life itself fades away.

249 Wild Nights – Wild Nights!

This is a passionate poem with clear references to sexual love. The *Wild Nights* of the title can be interpreted on at least three levels. The first level is developed in the nautical imagery of sailing on a wild sea and finding a safe harbour. The second level concerns a meeting and possibly consummation with a lover, developed through the ambiguity of words such as *luxury* (4), *Heart* and *port* (6), *Eden*, (9), and *moor* (11). The positive connotations of these words suggest a secure relationship. Thirdly, there is a possibility of a religious reading, with the speaker as a soul in the journey through life towards God in heaven. Once again an opposition is established: the sailing or searching, and the safe arrival in port.

The gender of the speaker is uncertain. Again Dickinson uses language from different registers in the same poem, to generate multiple levels of meaning. Images of nature are used to define sexual feelings, and might be seen to 'purify' references to sexual matters because these are natural and right. Images of sailing and nautical language are essential to the poem. Language drawn from a religious register is again used to express secular ideas, such as *Rowing in Eden* (9), as in 211: *'Come slowly – Eden!'* and 213: *'Did the Harebell loose her girdle'*.

When her editor, Thomas Higginson, first read this poem he refused to believe that his 'virginal' friend Dickinson would write a poem of a sexual nature, and he was afraid that readers might see 'improper' meanings in the poem. Nowadays, these are taken for granted. Another possible reading might suggest that Dickinson herself is the heart stranded in port, which could be an image of her isolation and inability to engage in love or love affairs.

This is a lyric with a strong, regular rhythm.

1 The poem opens with a typically striking first line. *Wild Nights!* is ambiguous, and the repetition, with the dash and exclamation mark, create an immediate sense of excitement.

2 The archaic word *thee* introduces the main idea of the poem and may suggest a prayer, but is open to several readings: a lover, a sailor's wife, perhaps the God to whom we or a sailor prays. A solemn tone attaches to this word.

4 The word *luxury* indicates how much this meeting is desired; it is a feminine rhyme paired with *thee* (2) and *be* (3), which are full masculine rhymes: might this be chosen to indicate the meeting of two genders, man and woman, mimicking one of the layers of meaning of the poem?

5–11 The punctuation of excitement gives way to a series of dashes, perhaps mirroring the sense of long searching or travelling.

7–8 The repetition of *Done with* creates an impression of the joy and relief of being safely in *port*. This sequence could also have other connotations of exploration and discovery; there might even be a sexual connotation of physical exploration of a body – this would be very much in the style of John Donne's love sonnets, which Dickinson knew.

9 The word *Eden* suggests the perfect place to be, a place of reward, peace and safety, and pulls together all of the meanings of the poem, secular and religious.

10 The assonance of the soft 'i' and 'e' sounds used throughout the poem creates a calmly confident tone which comes to a head in this line. The long-drawn-out and heavily stressed

phrase suggests that the journey through mysterious and difficult circumstances is over.

10/12 The final full, masculine rhyme of *Sea* and *Thee* brings closure to the poem, and the return of the exclamation marks create a sense of climax.

254 'Hope' is the thing with feathers

This is one of Dickinson's so-called 'Poems of Definition', in which she sets out to define an abstract quality by using physical and natural examples. The poem again rests on two opposing factors: there is the metaphorical bird and the underlying abstract meaning about the virtue of hope.

The poet praises the value and power of hope by using the image of a brave, determined little bird. The poet details the hostile conditions which do not stop the bird from singing. It is suggested that the power of hope lies within us all, needing no support or consideration: it will surface to help us whenever circumstances require it. Again Dickinson presents an idea with a religious root in a secularized way. Traditionally, Christians believe in three central virtues: faith, hope and charity.

This appears to be an unusually cheerful poem with no darkness; although life's problems are mentioned in the form of the *storm*, the tone is wholly optimistic. It is a straightforward lyric poem with a regular, tuneful rhythm. The dashes create enjambment, so that the whole poem is a single thought with no breaks, just as the strength of hope will never be broken. The frequent alliteration of 's' sounds creates a musical, gentle tone to suit the subject matter of this optimistic poem.

1 Immediately the writer names the subject matter with the opening definition; the use of quotation marks stresses this. To begin with, the writer draws attention to the bird's feathers; perhaps to suggest the fragile power of the bird as it soars into the sky. Perhaps this metaphor suggests that difficulties may seem burdensome, but they can be borne.

3 The writer uses the word *And* repeatedly in the poem, to stress the continuity of hope. The bird sings a *tune without the words*; is this meant to be an example to us? Might the idea of the song be used to suggest that we should remain optimistic, and the lack of words suggest that this advice can be applied in any circumstances?

9 As if to illustrate the moral lesson, the speaker intrudes into the poem: *I've heard it*. The use of the phrase *chillest land* suggests a moral or spiritual dimension where other emotions are frozen.

10 The phrase *strangest Sea* might suggest situations never experienced before.

11–12 The metaphor of the bird is finally developed in the last lines of the poem, where the bird *never... asked a crumb*.

258 There's a certain Slant of light

This lyric poem is written in a very different mood from the previous poem. The speaker/observer watches the landscape, which is initially described, but this gives way to an account of the landscape of the mind. Both are merged in the last stanza.

Watching the shaft of light over the landscape, the speaker undergoes a change of mood, experiencing some sort of inner vision which leads to considerations about the human condition. The oblique shaft of light falls as heavily on the speaker's mind as bells from a great cathedral, bringing about a brief transformation. The four separate stanzas reflect the changes of focus within the poem. The landscape is described in stanza 1; in stanzas 2 and 3 the mind of the speaker is the focus; and in the last stanza the speaker's mind is projected on to the landscape and both are merged.

The speaker seems to be quiet, isolated and even alien to us and to nature, waiting for something. There is a sense of loneliness and isolation, with the idea of change and mutability brought into the last stanza. There seems to be a comment about decay, like the oblique passing light, in the world of man. There is little consolation for the speaker, little relief from an oppressive bleakness. Perhaps the writer wants us to move beyond the personal and individual and think about the loneliness of human life and ways in which we might combat this. There is a sense of awe as if the speaker and we are waiting, listening and hoping for something. But nothing happens, and the wait is in vain – there is no message from heaven. You will see a similar motif in 465: '*I heard a Fly buzz – when I died*'.

There is another possible reading based upon the shaft of light. According to Christian belief the Paraclete, or Holy Spirit, the third person of the Trinity, was the bringer of wisdom to the apostles. In religious paintings this was portrayed as a shaft of light falling upon a person, bringing enlightenment and wisdom. This would add a level of irony to the meaning of this poem, although Unitarians would disapprove as they did not believe in the Trinity.

3 **Heft** a load-bearing part of a cathedral structure, such as a pillar. The use of this noun brings the sense of touch into the poem.

4 The sound of the cathedral bells creates an aural image which is typical of Dickinson's use of devices, as also in 280: '*I felt a Funeral, in my Brain*'.

10 The *Seal* represents the sacraments with which Jesus promised salvation, in Calvinist belief. Dickinson turns this reference on its head as *Despair* replaces any sense of hope. The image of the *Seal* develops the meaning of the poem further. A *Seal* implies the signature of a document, but also there is the religious connotation; God gave the sacraments as a promise or 'Seal' to the Elect who would go to heaven. Is there a promise in this poem? Although there is waiting, nothing really comes. Yet again you see Dickinson divorcing religious language and tropes from their roots, applying them to nature and to the mind of man. She again places her trust in things of the earth rather than of heaven.

11 The word *imperial* suggests a powerful and almost irresistible force.

13–16 The writer uses personification in describing the landscape and creates suspense on the reader's part. The use of dashes, helps further to create a mood of waiting, watching and perhaps hoping.

280 I felt a Funeral, in my Brain

This poem appears to include the account of a funeral; mourners tread as they walk past the coffin to say their goodbyes and take their seat at the service. This is followed by the interment when the coffin is placed in the grave, but there is a moment of horror when a plank holding the coffin breaks, and it plunges into the abyss of the grave that has been dug.

On one level the *I* of the poem could be the dead person recalling her own funeral. Other readers see this poem as an account of a person going mad, as the last *Plank in Reason* breaks. Perhaps this person becomes unconscious; or it could be that the person reaches a new, higher area of consciousness to which we ordinary readers cannot gain access. Perhaps the poem is autobiographical, about Dickinson herself when she endured one of her mental 'terrors'; or it might be about anybody who experiences a breakdown. All of these readings are possible and come together at the end of the poem.

Some readers point out the Gothic elements in this poem. Dickinson had read Edgar Allan Poe, who wrote a story about a mind breaking down, *The Fall of the House of Usher*. Elements of this genre include the use of a female victim (although this is not certain as we do not know the gender of the speaker); suspense, built up by the repetition of words and phrases; the church/graveyard setting; the tolling of the bell; the yawning, open grave; the changes in the state of consciousness of the speaker; the powerful sound effects. All of these effects could be seen to create a chilling atmosphere. There could be also links to the American Civil War as Dickinson had already lost acquaintances and friends.

Again the poem rests on a contrast, between the person apparently dying and those who are living. At the end of the poem, as in 79: '*Going to Heaven!*' and 216: '*Safe in their Alabaster Chambers*', there are no references to salvation and resurrection, and no sense of a consoling religion.

1 How does one 'feel' a funeral in the brain as opposed to the senses? In this poem the senses, except for hearing, are confused or destroyed as the poet employs synaesthesia (a confusion of sense impressions); this provides a brilliant and puzzling start to the poem. Perhaps this suggests that the poem will be about both an inner and an outer experience. Seemingly incongruous ideas are pulled together. The gender of the persona is uncertain.

2/4 To Dickinson, *fro* and *through* would have rhymed for emphasis.

3 The use of dashes throughout, along with the use of enjambment, help to create an ongoing, unstoppable movement.

3–7 The repetition of *treading* with the half-rhyme on *breaking*, and further repetition of *beating*, enact the sound of the mourners walking round the coffin; do these also evoke the sense of a heart still beating, perhaps in terror?

4 The idea of *Sense… breaking through* suggests the oppression evident in 258: *'There's a certain Slant of light'*.

10 The reference to the soul draws on a religious register, but again, there are no further references to suggest a Christian poem. The metaphor in *creak across my Soul* is another metaphysical image of oppression and injury.

13 Aural effects come to a climax.

14 Throught synecdoche, human life is now reduced to an ear, as in 211: *'Come slowly – Eden!'* there was simply a pair of lips.

16 The words *Wrecked* and *solitary* again suggest total isolation and destruction. There is no sense of restoration after death.

17 Already the word *And* has begun six lines of the poem. In the last stanza this word starts every line, perhaps to sound like the tolling of the funeral bell or to stress the inevitability of the unstoppable plunge into the final dark abyss of the grave, or madness. *Reason* is breaking down; is there any possibility that there might be another, perhaps a higher sort of knowledge to be gained after death, so that there might be some kind of optimistic outcome after all?

288 I'm Nobody! Who are you?

Readers see many different readings of this apparently simple little poem, in which the speaker seems to ask the reader for his or her credentials in a form of greeting. If you remember that Dickinson herself came from one of the leading families in Amherst you will find a certain irony in the poem's first line. However, there are several ways in which the idea of being *Nobody* can be interpreted.

Some readers find the poem to be pretentious and that Dickinson is putting on a front to justify her strange behaviour socially. Her isolation, withdrawal from society and strange clothing could be seen as a form of humility, according to readings that rest on autobiography. There could be another autobiographical reading that sees the poem as a typically ironical, light-hearted account of her refusal to be published and to seek fame.

Others see a political element in this poem; it might be seen as a criticism of those who try to gain popular approval. In this version, the frog would be the loud-mouthed politician who is loud and vulgar in his or her attempts to gain power or popularity. Dickinson was known to be politically conservative, approving of the older, more aristocratic ways, and it has been suggested that the frog represents the modern democratic orators who speak loudly, even if effectively, at public meetings.

Related to this meaning there is another about class structure. The poem could be written to express sympathy for the many citizens of America who had no status, and were oppressed and voteless, officially not existing. These people included certain ethnic groups such as black and native Americans, and immigrants such as the Irish. However, there could be a less attractive meaning related to this last reading. Instead of sympathy, the poem could reveal a contempt for the Irish 'bog-trotters' who swarmed into the States to make their way in that society. According to this reading, *Nobody* might imply someone who is too educated, wealthy and cultured to belong to the *admiring Bog* which is captivated by the *Frog*. So the poem could be seen as an invitation to others sharing her views and social/cultural standing to align with this viewpoint.

A very modern reading could be to see this poem as an attack on the vulgar pursuit of 'celebrity', which is now so dominant. However, all these readings stand together, and it is probably true to Dickinson's temperament and fear of fame to accept it as partly autobiographical. She was afraid of going into print, and this is expressed clearly in 709: '*Publication – is the Auction*'. She was known to have disliked all types of public oratory, as in 303: '*The Soul selects her own Society*' and 315: '*He fumbles at your Soul*'. In this light, the poem becomes cheerful and teasing.

1 The poem opens with the speaker making a direct address to the reader, asking direct questions. There seems to be an ironic contradiction in writing *Nobody* with a capital letter. Doesn't this imply that *Nobody* is actually a name for somebody?

1/2 The full masculine rhymes of *you/Too* matched with the half-rhyme of *know* in line 4 give the poem a sense of confidence and certainty to support the meaning.

2 The use of dashes perhaps suggests that the speaker is asking coded questions, and the reader is meant to fill in the meanings.

6 The simile of the frog opens up the meanings of the poem. To most people, a frog is an ugly creature that makes a lot of noise. Could this image relate to all types of public speaking, secular and religious?

6/8 Again the full rhymes of *Frog* and *Bog* reinforce the liveliness of the poem and the certainty of the message.

7 The phrase *the livelong June* is a colloquialism, perhaps used to engage the reader. June, as midsummer, is used perhaps to suggest a person in the prime of life, full of energy and vigour; or perhaps it is the season when everything is at its best. This might help convey the vigour and liveliness of the poem and also of the speaker.

8 Most readers see *admiring* as ironical, casting doubt on the mental, cultural and social status of the bog-dwellers. The word *Bog* opens up the political and class-related readings of the poem.

303 The Soul selects her own Society

This poem might be related to 288 above, in the sense that it is open to a class-based reading in which Dickinson shows awareness of her background and high social status. The speaker chooses to be open to just a chosen few and exclude everyone else. The tone is confident, and again this could be autobiographical. Fear of social change and increasing democracy could be evident, as in 585: '*I like to see it lap the Miles*'. In this sense, the poem could be an apology for, or explanation of, the way Dickinson conducted her life.

The poem could also be read as an account of the soul, remote from and undisturbed by the external world; it sees all that is going on, but is unmoved by any worldly activity. The speaker presents the soul as a woman in her own home, safe and secure. She chooses her own company and closes the door on most people, the *divine Majority* who form her potential society and who would like her to join them. Ceremony does not impress her as she rejects the grand chariots that briefly stop at her door; even the emperor who kneels at her feet will be denied. These images suggest that she does not want worldly things such as popularity, wealth, power or position. Again, there is a strong autobiographical echo here. The speaker then continues by revealing that the soul has been confronted with a choice of many people, the *ample nation*, but has chosen one and paid no attention to anyone else.

The poem works on two levels: first there is the domestic language and imagery of the contented woman in her home. Dickinson rejects normal views of power; neither fame nor power matter to her. She is as a woman complete and fulfilled in her isolation, with just the one person whom she has chosen. Could this one person be Poetry?

Then there is the strong religious element of the poem, particularly in the language of election and selection. Puritans believed that there was a group of people called the 'Elect'; these were worthy people free of sin whom God had chosen for salvation. This is translated in the poem into the soul making the selection, not God. Also the speaker suggests that the soul was free to reject all of the *divine Majority*. Dickinson goes much further here than in previous poems that use religious imagery for secular purposes, such as 211: '*Come slowly – Eden*' and 214: '*I taste a liquor never brewed*'. Here she reverses religious doctrine in ways that might be shocking to Puritans. The speaker, not God, has written the doctrine.

1 The use of dashes here and throughout the poem creates a sense of ongoing thought.

1–4 *Society/Majority* introduces feminine rhyme, which is balanced by the masculine rhyme of lines 2 and 4; perhaps in terms of gender this suggests completeness. The rhymes here differ from the rest of the poem, perhaps to create an initial tone of harmony. In the rest of the poem the rhymes are mostly half-rhyme or feminine rhyme, perhaps to support the contemplative tone.

2 Introduces the domestic imagery of the house and door.

3 The religious theme is evident in *divine Majority*. There is also a suggestion of political jargon.

5 From this point onwards in the poem there is an alternation of long and short lines; perhaps this enacts the theme of the poem, that from a huge nation just one lives alone, or will select just one other being.

5/7 The word *Unmoved* is repeated for emphasis, in a heavily stressed position at the start of a line.

6 The *low Gate* might be a religious reference. The door to the stable where Jesus was born was low, and the kings, shepherds and other visitors had to stoop to enter. This is replicated in some shrines today. The word *low* might suggest humility, or might be used in a biblical sense rather irreverently to point out the significance of the speaker's soul.

9 The speaker intrudes, with *I*; might this support an autobiographical reading? The past tense here in the word *known* may create some ambiguity of meaning. Has the 'I' persona made such a choice in the past, and is the persona now living in harmony with the selected one? Or was this choice

made in a past episode now finished, so the persona now lives alone? The use of the word *ample* stresses how many people there were to choose from, and how limited a choice was made.

11 *Valves* is a complex word which creates several layers of meaning. The reference could be to the valves of the heart; in the past, doors had valves, which were a type of hinge to allow them to fold (this also ties in to the image of the woman closing the door). Valves are also used in machines or engines to control the flow of liquids such as oil or petrol; this could tie in with Dickinson's dislike of modern society with its technology. The hardness of the word could be a preparation for the harsh-sounding end of the poem.

12 The word *Stone* is a hard-sounding one; it is a half-rhyme, a masculine rhyme with *One*. The word sounds weighty and final, suggesting that the choice made is deliberate and final. The ending of the poem is not gentle; it leaves the reader wondering whether the isolation was indeed truly out of choice, or was enforced; again, this taps into an autobiographical reading of the poem. The last dash leaves the poem open-ended: as though this isolation is ongoing.

315 He fumbles at your Soul

This poem is a highly concentrated account of a man. All the readers know about him is that he is skilled in controlling his audience. Who is he? We do not know; he could be a preacher, an actor, a lover, or God. On a more abstract level he could be what we know Dickinson feared, a powerful male engaged in the politics of gender and sex; other readers think that he could be Reverend Charles Wadsworth, or one of the new breed of dynamic young preachers.

However, the speaker/observer watches him closely, knowing how calculating he is, exactly how he manipulates, and the effects he wishes to create. The audience is seduced, then stunned and then scalped. It seems unlikely that the speaker has been taken in, as the overall portrait is quite amusing.

The poem is seen to act in the same way as the 'sermon' itself; the reader is fascinated, captivated, brought to boiling point, and allowed to cool before the last *Thunderbolt*. In this way it is a kinetic poem, one full of vigour. Where does the *Thunderbolt* come from? From the power of the preacher, or God? All we know, and the use of dashes makes this clear, is that it is all calculated and controlled.

The last two lines are set apart, and the writer moves to the plural word *Winds*. What might this suggest? Are there more out there like him? Although the speaker/observer has successfully stood firm against him this time, what about the end of the poem? The final dash denies closure; does that suggest that it is likely to happen all over again?

1 The metaphor of *fumbles at your Soul* offers a startling opening; the verb is tactile and normally would be related to something concrete. Again Dickinson is using concrete imagery to express abstract ideas.

2–3 The man is certainly a player in many senses of the word; the *Keys* suggest piano-playing, but also locks. Is he seeking entrance to an area normally forbidden? This line introduces the first main metaphor of the poem, that of music as a vehicle of entrancement, which increases until it is *full*.

4 The adverbial phrase *by degrees* indicates the movement of the poem as intensity grows; the sequence of verbs and nouns intensifies.

6 The word *Ethereal* is puzzling; has it come from the heavens? Has the preacher a heavenly gift? Is it used ironically?

7–10 The combination of dashes, the echo in *fainter/further*, the repetition of *Then* and of *Your* all combine to give the sense of approaching menace.

9–10 There is a break in the process, but no respite. The repeated sounds in *Breath* and *Brain*, with the parallel line structure, are hypnotic and disturbing, as are the dashes and alliteration of 'l'.

11–12 The power structure between speaker and listeners has changed completely. There is a sense of helplessness in the nakedness of the soul; the dashes suggest control and also the finality with which the blows are delivered. The man's force is now brutal and overwhelming: *imperial*. The word *scalps* is striking; Dickinson once wrote to her editor Thomas Higginson that she recognized poetry when it took the top of her head off. Might the brutal force also be the act of reading or writing poetry?

13–14 The last two lines are offset away from the body of the poem; why might this be? There is a complete change of metaphor and register to the natural world. Again Dickinson uses natural imagery to convey human emotions, as in 213: *'Did the Harebell loose her girdle'* and 249: *'Wild Nights – Wild Nights!'*. Perhaps the *Winds* suggest human beings shaken to their core; there are *Paws*, but why? Might this suggest the animal brutality of the speaker, and the way he toys with his audience? The use of dashes suggests slowing down to the point of standstill, but the final dash leaves the poem without closure.

322 There came a Day at Summer's full

This poem is about a single joyful day when the speaker was with her lover. However, the perfect day passes all too quickly and they must part and suffer until they are finally reunited after death in heaven. The poem is a perfect example of how Dickinson used religious tropes and language to express secular ideas about human love.

The religious background is rather complex. In Puritan theology, particularly in Calvinism, there were just two sacraments (holy rites of the church): baptism and the Lord's Supper, remembered in the sacrament of Communion and the taking of bread and wine. Partaking of sacraments places the soul in a state of grace, ready to go to heaven. These were created by Jesus as a promise or 'Seal' to mankind that one day they would be redeemed and would be resurrected in heaven if they were free of major sins. The reference to the 'Seal' also suggests the 'covenant' or 'contract' made with mankind through the crucifixion, by which Jesus promised salvation to the worthy. All would then partake of the 'Supper of the Lamb' (the Lamb is another name for Jesus). But to Calvinists, only certain people, the Elect, would be predestined for heaven, chosen from the Divine Majority which was free of sin.

In the first stanza the speaker expresses her happiness, the day seeming to exist for her alone. In stanza 2, time is seen to pass very quickly, and the day passes without talking (stanza 3). In stanza 4 Dickinson uses complex religious imagery to express their closeness, and in stanza 5 the time of separation comes all too quickly. Dashes are used to indicate time passing, especially in the stanzas 5, 6 and 7. They know that each will suffer as much as the other (stanza 6) until they are re-united in heaven, which they will have deserved because of their suffering. The poem is an account of a very intense experience conveyed using religious references. These references have been secularized. For Dickinson, heaven is not a place to be with God, but with her lover, a continuation of earthly delights, as in 79: '*Going to Heaven!*' and 214: '*I taste a liquor never brewed*'.

There could be autobiographical roots to this poem; it was written in 1860, the same year as Reverend Charles Wadsworth, with whom it was rumoured the poet fell in love, visited Dickinson at Amherst.

1 The phrase *Summer's full* suggests that just as summer was at its height, so was the love between the lovers.
4 Resurrection is when the dead arise and go to heaven, achieving all that Jesus had promised and that they had waited for. This metaphor conveys how important the meeting was for the speaker.
7 The word *soul* anticipates the religious language of the poem. The *solstice* is the longest, as in this poem, or the shortest day of the year.
8 An image of growth describes their blooming love.
9 The significant religious imagery begins here. Just as people do not talk when taking Communion because it is a sacred moment, so these lovers see their love as a sacrament.
12 **Wardrobe** a metaphor for the sacraments.
13 **The Sealed Church** an image of the 'Elect' to be saved; the two lovers become the 'Elect' because of their fulfilled love, which is their own sacrament in this moment of being in heaven while on earth.

13–16 The speaker suggests that the lovers can share this moment of being together as a practice for the real 'Supper of the Lord' in heaven when they will finally be together. Unusually there is a suggestion that the speaker has some belief in the Christian faith. The full stop at the end of the stanza marks the end of their happy and holy time together.

17 There is a change of tone here. The word *Hours* is repeated to stress that time passes quickly and always will.

18–19 The lovers begin to fade into the distance; to show this, Dickinson refers to just hands, then simply two faces (a use of synecdoche as in 211: '*Come slowly – Eden!*'), as if on boats sailing away from each other.

23 The crucifix is used as an image of the cross upon which Jesus suffered and died.

24 The lovers were not engaged or contracted to marry. The bond was a spiritual bond of love.

25 Their *troth* or pledge lies in the fact that they will be resurrected together because of love.

27–28 They will then have their marriage in heaven, justified by their *Calvaries*. Calvary was the place where Jesus was crucified, and is used as a metaphor for suffering on earth. Some readers suggest that the poem may have been written about Reverend Charles Wadsworth, the man named as one of her possible lovers. He went away to a church called 'New Calvary'. Perhaps the word *Love* in the last line is meant to sound hopeful. The final dash again leaves the poem open-ended.

327 Before I got my eye put out

Initially this poem seems to be about going blind, as the speaker of this dramatic monologue appears to have been violently blinded in one eye. The speaker thinks about seeing all the things he or she used to see: the sky, mountains, birds and the gleaming road. However, this memory was prefixed with *But* (5); if told that he or she could see all these things again, the news would be fatal. It would appear that in the last stanza the speaker accepts fate, and decides that it is in fact safer to see with the soul.

There is obviously a link between seeing and owning, made evident in the repeated word *mine*; a Transcendental view of nature would claim that to see the natural world would be to own it. However, Dickinson does not seem to share this philosophy and denies possession. In a sense you do own things when you see them because they become part of your consciousness. The long list of possessions linked in the *mine* sequence might suggest that this richness is too much for the speaker – that withdrawal to an inner vision is the only way to live.

Dickinson had problems with her eyes, culminating in two visits to specialists at Boston. But this poem seems to go far beyond just personal experience. Some readers believe that the poem was prompted in part by her reading of Charlotte Brontë's *Jane Eyre*, and that this is a dramatic monologue written for the character of Mr Rochester. Perhaps so, and there are other literary echoes. Dickinson read John Milton, a great Puritan poet who went blind and wrote about the ironies of inner light and outer darkness. Teiresias, a character from Greek drama, was blind, but a great prophet. Perhaps Dickinson taps into the tradition that the prophet sees only through inner light. Is she considering the role of the poet as prophet and visionary? Her own withdrawal from society would support this idea; to see too much of nature and of society, which might well be symbolized in this poem by the road, would kill her. In fact, might that road be one of the key symbols of the poem, in a debate about which road the speaker/poet/Dickinson herself should take? Might that be why the surface is described as precious *Amber*?

The poem, like 280: '*I felt a Funeral, in my Brain*', follows the Gothic tradition with its implied violence, perhaps a female victim, darkness, isolation and a mysterious atmosphere. Against this background Dickinson sets up one of her characteristic oppositions, based on words related to the register of light and seeing: *I*, *eye*, *sky* and *Mountains* throughout the poem contrast to the loss of sight. Typically, a paradox is established in which light does not bring vision, but darkness illuminated by the inner soul does. As the *eye* disappears, so does the *I*. Again typically, Dickinson uses synecdoche as in 211: '*Come slowly – Eden!*' and 322: '*There came a Day at Summer's full*', so that all that is left of the speaker is the soul, which awaits inner visions against the window pane.

Was a decision made to see with the light of the soul, and has the persona carried out the blinding in line 1 himself or herself? Metaphorically the question is whether the speaker made the decision to live by a different light, and this in itself caused the rejection of outer vision. Was this an active choice? Has the speaker, or Dickinson herself, deliberately moved from being an observer of society to becoming a prophet for society?

1 The usual startling opening to the poem captures attention. The interplay of *I* and *eye* begins and is resolved at the end of the poem.

4 The *other way* will be revealed at the end of the poem as the light of the soul.

7 The sequence on possession starts, underlined by the repeated use of *mine*, which goes on until line 16, and the use of dashes.

8 To see all this would kill the speaker; repeated for emphasis in line 17.

15 **Amber** a valuable fossil mineral used for jewellery; the value suggests the value of the sight now lost. The reference to the *Road* brings in the idea of society; also meaning 'route', this word may hint at the choice the speaker will make.

17 The reference to death abruptly ends the list of sights/possessions. The masculine half-rhyme of *Road/dead* emphasizes this finality, as do the harsh consonant sounds.

18 The decision has been made so a new, softer sound with alliteration on 's' supports a change to a quieter tone. An aside to the reader with the word *guess* (indicated by dashes) emphasizes the thought that has gone into this decision.

20 **put their eyes** an unusual way of saying 'look'; perhaps this is to stress that the author was initially happy with this mode of vision.

21 *Incautious* is heavily stressed at the start of the line. It is suggested that the speaker was blinded by the *Sun*; perhaps this might suggest being blinded by the beauty and wonder of the world.

328 A Bird came down the Walk

This seems to be a straightforward narrative poem in which an observer watches a bird eat, drink, hop and then fly away.

The poet records this in tiny detail, even down to the way the bird bites the worm in two and eats it *raw*. This may make the reader shudder, but that is the world of the bird. While unafraid of the beetle, he is *frightened* by the approaching human, so flies off. The last stanza has a vision of the natural world, with oceans and butterflies.

Dickinson was to some extent a Romantic poet, but she held no sentimental views of nature, believing that the worlds of man and nature are alien to each other. The bird eating the worm is entirely natural, even if distasteful to humans; he has a shared code with other creatures, stepping aside to allow a beetle to pass. Even the grass helps by offering him a *convenient* drink. Is the bird really afraid? All the evidence of fear is attributed by the speaker. It is the speaker who thinks he moves like one in danger, but is this true? The image of *frightened Beads* is odd; can a bead be frightened? Or has the image no validity? Is it actually the speaker who is *Cautious*? The reference to *Velvet* is conventional, as if the speaker has limited ideas about the creature that flies *softer home*; there is no sense of panic in this adverb.

However, as the bird flies into his natural dimension the poem becomes very much more sensuous. The ocean is even more silver, hence more valuable than a mining seam of silver; butterflies seem to leap and swim beside *Banks of Noon*. Might this be a view of the world from the bird's perspective? Or might Dickinson be suggesting through the speaker that what we can know about nature is very limited? *Banks of Noon* might refer to clouds, shadows, or flowers; but how can a butterfly leap and swim? A fleeting vision of a world of wonders to which only the bird has access might suggest that there is a wonderful dimension about which humans can know little. In that sense, offering a crumb to the bird is ironical; it is as if in return the bird has allowed the speaker a brief glimpse into a world from which human beings are debarred.

The tone is casual, yet by careful repetition (anaphora) of He and And, precise detail is created; this seems to be a moving picture of a bird. The fairly regular rhyme helps to create a conversational tone and the dashes support this, particularly in line 11, where they create an aside.

9 An apparent change of pace is signalled by the word *glanced* supported by *rapid*; the alliteration on 'd' mimicks the quick movements of the bird.

10/12 The sequence of actions with *hurried* and *stirred* adds to the quickening pace.

17–20 The repetition of the 'o' sound and the alliteration on 's' draws the last stanza together.

20 The adverb *plashless* suggests the harmony of this world, where leaping butterflies swim soundlessly.

341 After great pain, a formal feeling comes

In this 'Poem of Definition', Dickinson explores reactions to pain: the state of shock, numbness and finally some relief. Again, this poem is based on contrasts of feeling. As in 254: '*"Hope" is the thing with feathers*', a psychological state is portrayed using concrete language and images. As in 327: '*Before I got my eye put out*', where just the soul remained, here the author is concerned with the mind alone.

The feeling is described as *formal*; what might be implied? Perhaps behaviour in formal circumstances is rather mechanized, not spontaneous or emotional. Perhaps Dickinson is suggesting that our responses to great pain numb the nerves and senses so that the responses seem detached and automatic. This is suggested in the first stanza where the *Nerves* are dead, the *Heart* is *stiff*. In stanza 2, the person walks mechanically. In the third stanza the speaker describes a leaden feeling. But there is a change at the second line of this stanza when the speaker explains that this will be remembered later, if the victim survives this present wretched state. However, even if the person survives the shock, there will be metaphorical death. This is presented in the last two lines as the person begins to freeze, goes into a coma or stupor, then lets go – perhaps of life.

The ending of this dark poem is ambiguous. *Letting go* does not necessarily mean giving in to death. More optimistically, the letting go could be of the memory of pain, or it could be that the speaker lets go the numbing responses. The final dash denies closure to the poem.

This poem may have some autobiographical links, since Dickinson suffered severe mental trauma, especially in the 'terror' of September 1861. The poem is a personal response to suffering in this case, but by using the speaker as an intermediary the poet distances herself, thus achieving universality.

2 The word *Nerves* begins the sequence of naming the body parts that are becoming numb. The simile *ceremonious, like Tombs* recalls a funeral service, but also the coldness and motionlessness of a body in the tomb. This is the change happening to the speaker.

3 The heart is becoming confused, losing track of time. The *He* could refer to Jesus, who died on the cross, perhaps looking to him as an example of enduring pain.

5 Wandering mechanically, the speaker has now lost any sense of purpose or control.

9 A *Quartz contentment* might suggest that the mind, once full of vitality, has turned to stone so appears contented or still. The simile *like a stone* repeats and emphasizes this image, but also perhaps the word *stone* picks up the *Tombs* image of line 2.

10 The *Hour of Lead* is the time of oppressiveness when the spirit is at its heaviest.

13 The dashes throughout the poem have locked the different phases together. In the last line each dash heralds a new state.

401 What Soft – Cherubic Creatures

Dickinson is skilled in her character sketches, as in 315: *'He fumbles at your Soul'*. Without much surface detail she nevertheless presents a very clear portrait. It has been suggested that her interest and skill in satire were partially developed through reading the novels of George Eliot, but a waspish humour is evident in many of her poems.

This poem begins on a light, mocking note, but ends with a much more serious moral comment. In the first stanza the ladies of society are compared to a soft, loose fabric – perhaps suggesting lack of character – and then to a star, perhaps suggesting that they are cold and remote. Dickinson reveals why she has contempt for these women; because they have contempt for any aspect of human nature which is not perfect – *freckled*. The irony is that the ladies do not see their own freckles. The ladies are emotionally and morally flimsy, like the *Dimity* or lightweight cotton dresses they wear. Their feelings are not natural; they are over-refined and pretentious. Importantly the writer suggests that they are even ashamed of God, which leads into the harsh criticism of the last stanza.

Here Dickinson is severe, and she uses a religious analogy to establish her criticism. They would see the *Degree* or social status of being a fisherman degrading, but Jesus's apostles were drawn from fishermen, and it is through him that redemption is possible.

1 The dashes help create a conversational tone, supported by the enjambment. The adjective *Soft* perhaps implies a lack of inner strength. The word *Cherubic* suggests that although the ladies might look as pretty as a cherub in a painting, there is something inappropriate in women being like babies.
2 The word *Gentlewomen* is heavily stressed to bring out the irony.
3 **Plush** a soft, velvety material with a deep pile, enforcing the image of softness.
4 **violate a Star** a complex phrase which brings out the beauty

and the coldness of the women. The idea of violation might suggest that these women are not human enough for healthy sexual relationships.

5 **Dimity** a fine, flimsy cotton material used for dresses.

7 The word *freckled* gives a gentle image of human nature with all its flaws, just as freckles are natural flaws in the complexion.

8 **Deity** God or the gods.

10 **Degree** social standing.

11 The word *Brittle* describes something that would break if stressed. This suggests the shallowness of these women.

414 'Twas like a Maelstrom, with a notch

This 'Poem of Definition' describes a period of intense mental trauma followed by relief. The poet concludes by wondering which was worse – the period of agony or the sudden relief from the torment. Was it better to have died than lived?

The poem has a dramatic opening in which the approaching trauma is described as a whirlpool drawing nearer and nearer. Whirlpools can suck a person in, and this whirlpool seems to have a notch, a little nick in which the poet becomes caught. Again, Dickinson uses natural imagery to define a psychological state.

The metonym of the *Hem* of a piece of clothing represents the speaker, perhaps suggesting that the speaker is female. The poem could be partly autobiographical, perhaps referring to the 'terror' of September 1861, or one of the psychological traumas that Dickinson experienced. Poems of Definition may well be her attempt to come to terms with and define her own experience.

The delirious mood marks the moment when the speaker is entrapped in the maelstrom, and the poet moves from the use of natural imagery to a dramatic episode in the third stanza where a *Goblin* – a supernatural being usually linked with evil and torment – coldly and calculatingly measures the hours until he grabs the speaker. Again there is use of the Gothic genre: female victim, darkness, foul weather, noise, and evil, supernatural forces. These effects create a melodramatic moment in the final two lines. There is a comparison where the *Second* of time the speaker has left is compared or weighed against the Goblin's *Hours*. This suggests fragility and insignificance, and the Gothic tradition is recalled.

In the fourth stanza the speaker stresses her helplessness as not only were her muscles failing, but she was going numb. Suddenly, God remembered the victim and the *Fiend* was vanquished. The speaker describes these feelings in the next stanza; she felt like a prisoner condemned to death being led out to be hanged. At that moment, facing execution, the body and mind freeze. In the dungeon there was at least the *luxury* of delay, perhaps even hope. The last stanza has a bittersweet tone. The speaker recalls feeling blinded, deprived of the sense of sight at the moment of execution, when suddenly a reprieve was given. Finally, the speaker wondered whether it would have been better to have died then after so much suffering than to live, attempt to recover and possibly face it all again.

The different modes of presentation, first the natural imagery of the maelstrom, then the dramatic, supernatural presentation of the goblin episode, offer no consistent tone to the account. But taken as psychological trauma, the reading is perfectly consistent. Another important aspect is the way religion is treated. God's act of remembering is punctuated by dashes as if to indicate that this was entirely by chance; he was both an indifferent and a forgetful God. There is no evidence of a caring God looking after mankind; instead it seems to be a matter of chance that the helpless victim survived at all.

1 **Maelstrom** a whirlpool.
2/4 The rhymes are mixed to present the confusion of the speaker.
3 **boiling Wheel** the foaming centre of the whirlpool.
6 **delirious Hem** a metonym used for compression.

10 **Goblin** a supernatural creature known for cruelty. Dickinson had read the poems of Christina Rossetti who presented Goblins similarly in *Goblin Market*.
16 Sometimes the devil is called the *Fiend*. In this sense the poem could be read as a struggle between good and evil in the speaker's mind.
20 The *luxury of Doubt* suggests a hope that there might still be a reprieve.
21 **Gibbets** structures upon which people are hanged.
22 The phrase *stitched your eyes* might suggest the speaker becoming blind and losing her senses. The active verb signifies perhaps the speaker's helplessness.
23 The *Creature* may be God, or might be a Goblin-like being. The speaker wouldn't know because she could not see.
25 The final question displays the indecision of the speaker.

441 This is my letter to the World

This is one of a group of poems in which Dickinson thinks about publication, printing and fame. Publication was the act of showing the poems to others, for example by sending them to friends.

This poem should ideally be read alongside 709: '*Publication – is the Auction*' and 754: '*My Life had stood – a Loaded Gun*' as all are related to Dickinson's debate about the role of the poet, printing and fame, and problems with marketplace values.

Many readers accept this poem as totally autobiographical; Dickinson wrote in isolation and was not successful in terms of public acknowledgement, such as that afforded to her contemporary fellow-Americans Nathaniel Hawthorne and Walt Whitman, and to British poets such as the Brownings. However it is untrue to say that the world, i.e. society, never wrote to or acknowledged the poet. About 12 poems were published in *The Springfield Observer* during her lifetime, and at least 500 had been sent to influential friends and family. But there was no great public acclaim. Perhaps it is worth remembering that Dickinson loved to assume roles; here there is the somewhat melodramatic and Romantic notion of the poet in her attic spinning out words all alone, established in the first two lines of the poem. However, ambiguity then creeps in. The suggestion might be that nature itself is revealing truths about Dickinson, or the meaning might be that the speaker is important as a poet because she is revealing truths about nature, which links in to the idea of poet-as-prophet of 327: *'Before I got my eye put out'*. Perhaps both meanings co-exist.

In the last stanza the mood is Romantic and almost sentimental. The poet thinks of unseen generations after her death receiving her poems. She makes a plea to the reader to *Judge tenderly* of her, perhaps because of her love of nature. There is no self-pity; instead the poet says, 'value my poems for their message, and not for the person who wrote them'. The plain diction and the hesitancy indicated by the dashes also help to avoid sentimentality.

This poem is a perfect example of Dickinson's use of common metre.

1 **World** society generally.
2 The phrase *never wrote* sounds almost like a lover's complaint.
2/4 The feminine rhyme of *Me/Majesty* helps to establish a quiet tone.
4 *Majesty* is attributed to nature and not to the humble poet.
8 The repetition of *Me* helps to ensure that the poet herself, and not her message (despite the plea for the opposite), is remembered.

444 It feels a shame to be Alive

This poem may have been written as an elegy on the death of a friend, Frazar Stearns, who died in the Civil War. The genre of elegy might set up certain expectations in the reader's mind, such as praise and consolation. But Dickinson refuses to compromise her ideals. When the poem was written, about 1862, the war was a year old and through the new medium of photography people saw images of the brutal carnage.

The first stanza appears to be conventional, with the living honouring the dead. However, in the following stanzas the focus moves on to the community and the demands made on the people. The remains of the soldier may be buried after he died fighting for liberty, but the word *Pawn* is ambiguous and suggests that he is involved in a power game (from the pawn in chess) as well as the meaning of a deposit paid against a purchase (suggesting economic and commercial interests). The third stanza emphasizes this latter meaning; the piles of bodies are piles of *Dollars*; war is ultimately about money, despite the human price the soldier paid *Sublimely*.

In the penultimate stanza, unusually the word *we* is used to place the speaker as part of the community taking responsibility for the soldier's death. The poet asks whether *we* are worth the price of dying for as a community, given the economic basis of war. Finally, the poet turns to a religious question; is there a God to make suffering and dying worthwhile? The answer seems to be no; it is the soldiers themselves who are the *Saviors* and *Divinity*. This is a very strange poem to present as a personal elegy, but it is rigorous and honest. Dickinson places war in a universal frame including history, religion, society and the self as part of the community. She suggests that the state is interested only in dollars, which mean power; there are no higher principles at work. The most noble, most divine creature is man as the sacrificial soldier. Religious language becomes the secular language of war and sacrifice. The elegy praises the divine universal soldier, while at the same time suggesting that war is pointless and unprincipled.

3 The soldier's head as he lies dead on the battlefield floor makes the *Dust* honoured to hold him.

5 **Stone** tombstone.

6 The Spartans of ancient Greece were great warriors.
8 **Pawn** the least valuable piece in a chess game, and also a deposit paid on property.
9 *Sublimely* suggests the high moral principles of the soldier, to be contrasted with the financial metaphors related to the state.
11 This line is a vivid simile comparing the bodies to piles of cash.
14–15 A pearl is a priceless, flawless jewel which may be dissolved in acid.
19 The term *unsustained* could be a critical one expressing the idea that the state fails to give enough support to its soldiers in war. Also, religion has failed in giving spiritual support.

446 I showed her Heights she never saw

This poem seems to be about a person, possibly a lover, being refused by a woman. It exists in two versions, with the later version changing the person from *I* to *He*. The speaker could be either male or female. A female–female relationship would suggest Dickinson's love for Sue Gilbert, and quite possibly the poem could have been written to or for her. The speaker could, however, be the male in a traditional heterosexual relationship.

The speaker is offering help to a less experienced person to allow her to reach the *Heights*. It is uncertain what the metaphorical *Heights* represent; they could be skills, such as writing or music, or some sort of knowledge, or they could be sexual. The speaker is persuasive, seeming unable to believe that he or she could be turned down. But the refusal comes. Might the *solemn glow* suggest that the second person is happier and steadier after refusing? Or might it suggest that the woman seems even more glowing, even more beautiful to the speaker as she refuses and withdraws?

Unusually the poem is enlivened by dialogue, which creates swift changes in mood and tone. The poem again has many Gothic effects; a powerful leading voice; darkness; lights glowing;

mysterious happenings at night. All help to build up the reader's curiosity about situation and outcome. The negative of *never* in the first line is picked up in the third line, *Not so*, which prepares the reader for the final *No*. The seeing but not seeing of the opening line creates a sense of illusion, as does the increasing glow as the woman withdraws.

Might the rope also support this idea of an illusionist's magic act? Is the speaker in the same way trying to trick her? Or might the rope be picking up the image of mountaineering in climbing the heights? Or might it be a rope strung across the sky to support the stars, in a romantic image? The idea of a rope might carry a sense of entrapment as well. Possibly all these meanings are engaged as all support and expand on the central idea of persuasion.

The use of italics for emphasis adds to the character sketch of the speaker. Clearly he or she cannot accept the refusal. The woman has been tempted by *Secrets* (5). However, *Morning's Nest* seems to be a secure domestic or natural image related to the human home, or the home of birds; but this might become sinister in line 6. The word *Guest* may be calculated to sound innocent, as a guest does not usually demand too much. But what is to be made of the *Secrets*? Might these be sexual? The word *Nest* might also carry a sexual reference to 'bed'.

At the end of the poem a light is seen to glow. Might this light be the unextinguished and in fact still growing love of the speaker for the woman? If it is assumed that the speaker is male and Dickinson is engaging in role-play, there is room for suggesting considerations of gender power. The poem could be, in that light, a sombre demonstration of how persuasive males can be, and how hard it is for a woman to extricate herself from a sexual advance.

Dickinson wrote the last three lines of the poem on a separate piece of paper pinned to the rest. This might suggest that she was uncertain of the outcome of the poem, and that the 'temptation' offered in the poem might have turned out differently.

4 The repetition of *me*, the question mark and the use of italics suggest the importance of this line and the speaker's determination.
5 The word *Secrets* might have sexual connotations, but could refer to any particular knowledge. *Morning's Nest* may be a natural image of sunrise, a domestic image of the bedroom, or a sexual image.
12 The question mark at the end suggests ambiguity. Is the shocked speaker simply repeating the refusal, or might the question mark imply hesitation, that next time she might not refuse? Or it could be a question addressed to the reader: 'Do **you** think that she finally said "No"?'.

465 I heard a Fly buzz – when I died

The poem is an account of a woman dying, presented from her own perspective. She describes the mourners waiting for something significant to happen. They are waiting; the tears are finished, the will has been made; all are prepared for the death. The mourners are waiting for something momentous, perhaps for Jesus to give a sign of salvation, but nothing happens. There is total flatness and a fly appears.

Rather as in 280: '*I felt a Funeral, in my Brain*', the female speaker is describing her own death in retrospect. The poem is coloured with aspects of the Gothic genre: death; suspense and stillness; tears and fears; a vivid use of the imagination; all topped by the grotesque image of the fly. Is it here that the greatest irony is evident? Instead of the king of heaven, a fly appears, perhaps the bluebottle type of fly that will produce the maggots which will eat her body. The mood changes are dramatic: hush, sorrow, and a sense of great anticipation are all debunked and denied in the anti-climactic (in some ways) entrance of the buzzing fly.

The poem is about death and there is no evidence of salvation. In many ways the poem is negative, although the black humour offsets this.

The beginning perhaps mocks the Puritan ritualization of death. The eyes of the people waiting are *wrung... dry* and their breathing is *gathering firm*; it is as though they are professional mourners who have performed the expected rituals. The speaker tells of how the watchers await Jesus; but the woman who is dying is thinking of practicalities such as making her will. Perhaps the soul and spiritual aspects are the *portions* that might not be signed away? Traditionally in Christian belief, the soul belongs to God; but the speaker is prevented from following this line of thought. Might this be because of doubts about salvation and resurrection? Or might it be that such a belief does not even enter the speaker's mind?

This doubt is grotesquely confirmed when instead of the *King* (7), the fly appears – *uncertain* and *stumbling*, rather like questions about faith. Any hope of divine confirmation disappears as the fly gets in the way of the speaker's *light*. Might the fly represent doubt and uncertainty? The windows appear to fail, giving no light – presumably natural light, but also the light of reason and the light of faith; the speaker cannot see anything at all. There is no hope, no promise; the windows to the soul become darkened. The poem ends without closure, indicated by the last dash, and this supports the theme of uncertainty and loss of direction.

In Dickinson's time there was a genre known as 'mortuary poetry', and there could be a satire against this genre here.

1 The dashes suggest casualness about death, which supports a theme; if there is no redemption then to a Christian, death is robbed of significance.

2/3 The repeated word *Stillness* linked in a simile, the use of dashes, and the alliteration on 's' create a quiet, intense atmosphere to be deflated by the end of the poem.

5 The *Eyes* belong to those gathering around the deathbed for the vigil. This was important to Puritans, who believed that a quiet, resigned death might indicate that the deceased was one of the 'Elect', so would be saved.

12 The fly is first mentioned incidentally, but the dash links it to the next stanza.

13 The sight (the colour blue) and the sound of buzzing take over the room. The buzz of the fly is *stumbling*; this adjective is usually used of speech or movement. There is a suggestion of synaesthesia, that the senses are becoming confused and merged as life fails.

14/16 The rhymes suggest a formal conclusion, with full masculine rhymes, compared to the half-rhyme of earlier stanzas.

15 The *Windows* are literally part of the room, but also metaphorically the windows onto the soul. The fly is linked with doubt and lack of vision; it seems to be the only certainty at the moment of death.

501 This World is not Conclusion

The beginning of this poem is a little deceptive, as in the opening lines Dickinson echoes the traditional Christian view that there is another world beyond earthly existence, even though it is *Invisible*. However, this poem is another in which Dickinson debates the existence of an afterlife.

She comments that this idea has baffled philosophers, wise men and scholars as a riddle would. In fact people have died for a belief scorned by their fellow men, just as Jesus did. However, according to believers, in his crucifixion Jesus provided the means for redemption and salvation.

Dickinson personifies faith as a person who slips and becomes lost. Rather mockingly she refers to the *Hallelujahs* (18) of those who sing loudly – perhaps too loudly – about their faith, but she dismisses this by ending on a note of scepticism: there will always be doubt.

In the second line of the poem the poet uses the word *Species*, which might be a reference to Charles Darwin's then fairly new, controversial book *The Origin of Species*, which cast doubt on the traditional account of creation in the Bible. This sceptical note is developed through the image of faith as neither secure nor robust. Asking a changeable weathervane the way is absurd.

The tone becomes openly mocking when the poet describes the Puritan congregation, with much noise and gesture, but little substance.

Karl Marx had not yet written that 'Religion is the opiate of the people' (meaning that religion is used to stop people from thinking about the reasons for their hardships), but Dickinson anticipates this image. Promises of rewards in an afterlife might help people to endure suffering or poverty in this life, so religion could act as a *Narcotic*, a sleeping powder or drug, manipulated by the state or the church to help maintain their control.

1 The opening line is presented as a complete sentence, suggesting certainty; but this is the proposition that the rest of the poem questions.

8 **Sagacity** wisdom.

16 **Vane** a weathervane, which swings around according to the direction of the wind.

19–20 Just as a drug may not be able to remove toothache, but the tooth continues to trouble the sufferer, so will doubt nibble or eat away at the soul. Again Dickinson uses a physical image to convey an abstract idea.

510 It was not Death, for I stood up

In this 'Poem of Definition', Dickinson uses strong oppositions such as *Frost* and *Fire* and alternative ways of attempting to define a psychological state by working through sensuous experience. By the end of the poem the definition of the mental state is even more elusive than at the beginning. The reader may understand something about the experience, but exactly what it was remains unclear. Again the poet uses concrete images to define an abstract condition.

The lines contrast standing up with lying down in death. Using the sense of sound, the speaker suggests that it must have been midday, as the bells *Put out their Tongues*, an aggressive and unsettling metaphor. But might they be funeral bells?

The sense of touch is used in the next stanza with *Frost* and *Fire* both experienced. There is synaesthesia as the sense of touch in stanza 2 merges into the tasting and seeing of the following stanza. Is the psychological trauma so great that the senses are failing? Is the speaker one of the line of dead bodies waiting to be buried?

A sense of entrapment is created in stanza 4, where the poet feels as though she is stretched on a rack, unable to breathe unless the *frame* pinning her is opened. There is now confusion of time as *Noon* becomes *Midnight*. The *And, And, And* sequence of the fourth stanza enacts this stretching and the mental agony being endured, one moment after another.

There is a breathless hush in stanza 5, where time has stopped and gives way to space. Personal identity is falling away, just as autumn frosts and winds kill summer's growth. However, the beating sound brings in an echo of the beating heart of the speaker – perhaps this is caused by terror? Perhaps the heart is about to stop.

But worse than this, might the whole universe be dead? The last stanza is noticeably different from the rest. Now there is a sense that the speaker is running out of energy, intellectually and physically, as the list of comparisons stops. As the dashes suggest, the words are not connected; an attempt to stop the trauma fails. There is a feeling of unstoppable chaos, of deadly chill; the final analogy uses the image of a shipwreck. There is nothing to hold on to, no sight of land. The speaker feels despair.

Perhaps it was despair that the poem was attempting to define. But it seems more likely that the speaker gives in to despair in the effort to define a mental state. This poem may well be autobiographical, written the year after Dickinson's 'terror' of 1861. To support this reading, there is a sense that the poet is trying to analyse an experience, which could lead to control over a psychological trauma. The attempt fails and the tortured mind gives up, as indicated by the closure at the end of the poem. This could be part of the high price Dickinson paid for her isolation and dislocation in pursuing her life as a poet. However, this isolation is ironically one of her greatest strengths as a poet as she is forced to look inwards, to focus on the human mind and psychological experience.

6 **Siroccos** hot, moist winds that blow in from the Sahara Desert across southern European countries.
13 **shaven** might suggest life becoming very constricted and constrained.
14 **fitted to a frame** suggests being stretched on the medieval instrument of torture, the rack.
19 The frosts are *Grisly* because they bring death to living things.
20 **Repeal** implies that the frosts undo all the goodness of summer growth.

512 The Soul has Bandaged moments

In this poem the poet thinks about the soul's alternating periods of freedom and joy, and of restraint and suffering. Again Dickinson uses concrete images to present a state of mind, and again the poem is based on oppositions. The first line is strikingly odd: how can the abstract soul endure such an experience? The image of *Bandaged* carries at least two meanings; it implies that there is a wound, but as bandages are tightly bound, it also suggests a feeling of constraint. In the course of the poem Dickinson contrasts restricted moments, or periods of time, presented in stanzas 1, 2 and 5, with the sense of freedom or escape in stanzas 3 and 4.

The soul is presented in a sexual image as a scared woman threatened by a *Fright*, possibly a demon or an evil man. As in 414: *''Twas like a Maelstrom, with a notch'*, the evildoer is characterized as a *Goblin*; in an image of rape, he sips the lips the lover has kissed. The rape is highly abstract, presented as a *thought so mean* attacking a *Theme – so – fair*.

The next two stanzas are happy, energetic and explosive; in the fourth stanza there is the sensuous image of the bee reaching his rose after long imprisonment, finding all he wants (his *Noon*), and being in heaven.

The image of a shackled criminal in the next stanza closes the period of freedom. The *plumed feet* ironically suggest either a bird or Hermes (Mercury), the messenger of the Gods. Horror returns, not to be spoken of.

The poem contrasts freedom with the pain of denial. The reference to the *thought* and *Theme* of stanza 2 might suggest that this is an analogy for the poetic mind, which needs freedom to create; the *plumed feet* could support this reading, as a poet could be seen as a songbird, or even as Hermes, the messenger bringing the knowledge of the gods to mankind. The *staples* in the *Song* perhaps imply the stopping of the poetic voice; the poet cannot sing now, merely *bray* like a donkey.

Perhaps this poem is autobiographical, representing Dickinson's response to the social and economic pressures that society imposes on her personally and representatively as a poet. There is a clear echo also of the disturbance created by war: the soul is described as being in a state of siege, seeks *Liberty*, which is dangerous, has the energy of a *Bomb*, and plunges back into horror. All of the images suggest the suffering of the poet in an unsympathetic, hostile society.

5 The *long fingers* carry sexual connotations, as does *Sip* in line 7. The dashes in this stanza, as in stanza 4, represent the slow pace of the seduction/lovemaking.

7 **Goblin** an evil, supernatural being.

13 The *Bomb* introduces war imagery into the poem.

18 *Noon* is the height of the day, representing the best of times. *Paradise* represents the state of perfection.

23 *Horror* is capitalized and personified, perhaps to represent a demonic figure.

528 Mine – by the Right of the White Election!

This is an ecstatic poem with the speaker in a state of rapture, as the exclamation marks make clear, and which the anaphora (repetition) of *Mine* emphasizes. Clearly the speaker has made a momentous decision and has achieved positive self-identity, but in which ways, and in what areas?

This is one of the clearest examples in Dickinson's poetry of divorcing religious tropes from their roots and applying them to the human psyche. Again there is the structuring of the poem as a series of oppositions. Words from the religious register include *Election*, *Seal*, *Sign*, and *Confirmed*; and from the language of religious ecstasy *Vision* and *Delirious*. These registers are set against the negative language of *Scarlet prison*, *conceal*, *Veto* and *Grave*. The opposition indicates that a choice has been made – perhaps autobiographically by the poet – and it is positive, enriching and liberating, which expels all negatives. The question is who has chosen what, and this of course is open to many meanings.

Perhaps the poem is autobiographical, as the year in which it was written, 1862, was part of Dickinson's most creative period. Perhaps she had learned from her friend Charles Wadsworth in his vigorous sermons how to relate religious language and experiences to everyday secular affairs. In a way, Puritanism was not oppressive to women since it was God, not man, who defined the 'Elect' who would go to heaven; gender was no barrier. So, full of confidence, the poet declares herself to be of the 'Elect'; it appears that she has usurped the role of God and elected herself. The *Seal* of the sacraments and of the covenant may represent an image of her poetry. Perhaps she has elected the art of poetry as her *Charter*, and is *Delirious* about this choice. The *Scarlet prison* might represent the heart and the emotions that make her choice inevitable. She is isolated, as if behind *Bars*, but her *Vision*, and her choice of writing topics, will be hers alone. She will therefore be in heaven while still on earth. In line 6 the reference to the *Grave's Repeal* might suggest that her name will be known after her death; the impact of death will be repealed, or cancelled out. (This theme links with 657: *'I dwell in Possibility'*.) In this particular reading, Dickinson is ecstatic about her chosen role and life.

It has also been suggested that there is a literary level of meaning (as in 327: *'Before I got my eye put out'*), derived from Nathaniel Hawthorne's novel *The Scarlet Letter*, to which Dickinson had a rather cool response. In the novel Hester Prynne, a young Puritan woman living in a closed society, is drawn into an affair with a preacher, Reverend Arthur Dimmesdale. She bears a child, Pearl, is shamed and is forced to wear the scarlet letter 'A', for adultery, on her breast; however, she survives, through intellectual and emotional strength. Finally Dimmesdale confesses, and dies, whispering to Hester that because of their guilt, they can never be together in heaven. This seemed to displease Dickinson, so it has been suggested that this poem was written as a dramatic monologue for Hester. The poem could represent Hester's claims for the rightness of the relationship. She had to wear a scarlet letter, but this did not break her spirit and she proclaims her moral vindication in this monologue.

Perhaps it could also be a statement of Dickinson's own love for her 'Master', defying the 'vetoes' of public opinion, and rapturously in love. The religious and sacramental language might suggest that her love is blessed and will outlast the grave. There is no marriage as such, but an election or choice; the scarlet heart is a sign of love – a love returned and confirmed, and above all a love that makes her *Delirious*.

The theme of whiteness is valid in all three readings; to Dickinson it might imply that she is personally unstained by social and economic struggles. Autobiographically, her view of herself was signified by her taking to wearing only white dresses. In the second reading the whiteness would be a deliberate contrast with the condemnatory scarlet letter, an image of Hester Prynne's inner purity. In the third, the whiteness could indicate the purity of her perhaps unconsummated love for her Master;

the whiteness might suggest the white heat of love, and also a wedding dress.

It is a vigorous, joyful poem made all the more striking by the strong rhythm, with nearly all lines carrying an initial stress; the anaphora of the emphatic *Mine!*; and the dashes creating anticipation, but also linking stanzas in a breathless rush of enjambment.

1 **Election** a reference to the Puritan belief that God will elect those people destined for heaven. This word also picks up language of the political register, which appears throughout her poems and includes here *Veto*, *Repeal*, *Confirmed*, and *Charter*. This register might be seen to underline the fact that this poem is about choice.
2 **Seal** to Puritans, Seals are the two sacraments given as a proof by God and as a promise of resurrection, and also the covenant that promises salvation.
5 **Veto** a prohibition.
8 **Charter** a set of legal rights, usually conferred upon a state, city or town.
9 The word *steal* suggests that time is quietly creeping by, but this does not affect the speaker.

585 I like to see it lap the Miles

This is one of Dickinson's best-known poems, often anthologized. It appears to be a cheerful, positive account of a railway locomotive, perhaps partly prompted by the opening of the Amherst line of the great railway in 1853.

The train is described on its journey as it destroys and devours, *laps* and *licks* everything along the way. It stops for water, goes round a mountain and straight through a quarry, noisily hooting, until it arrives punctually at its shed. There is a sense of fun, perhaps in the wordplay on the train as the 'iron horse', as it was known in the nineteenth century; but there is perhaps a critical undertone.

The poet reminds the reader of what the train has replaced – the horse-drawn carriage. So as well as being presented as a riddle, the poem gives a sustained image of an animal feeding, having ribs like a horse, crawling, neighing and being *docile* returning to his *stable*.

But what sort of animal is the new horse of the nineteenth century? Words of a negative register suggest doubt. The train devours the countryside, it is *prodigious* – perhaps too powerful? Has the countryside been quarried and blown open to allow the train to travel through? It might represent certain aspects of the modern age, appearing *supercilious* as it looks down on the poor in shanties. Such people would never be able to afford the luxury of train travel; it merely noisily pollutes their environment. It might seem to be *docile*, but it is all-powerful. There is a comparison to Boanerges, the sons of the god of thunder who brought suffering on all those who did not make them welcome. Boanerges is also a name for a fiery preacher, just as the engine makes fire. Might this be a hint of the dangers of industrialization, as past rural traditions are destroyed?

The metallic clickety-click sound of wheels on welded railway lines is echoed in the 'l/k' sounds of the first two lines. The rhythm is common metre, but this is disturbed in the second stanza and at the beginning of the third. At lines 9 and 10 there is a sense of the tightness of the track through the quarry, as the short lines indicate slowing down to squeeze through. There is full enjambment, so that the poem speeds along in one unbroken sentence to mimic the journey. The dashes help create continuity, indicate a detour in line 7, and emphasize the exclamation of *horrid* in line 12. The end of the poem is ironic; the comparison to the star might remind the reader that nature has no place in a technological society. The *docile* aspects of the locomotive are negated by the use of the word *omnipotent*. There is some sense of danger or of a threat, which is quite in keeping with the fact that Dickinson ran away from the opening of the Amherst railway in 1853.

3 **Tanks** along the tracks, tanks hold water which is used to make steam to drive the engine.
5 A *Pile of Mountains* is a not very elegant 'train's-eye view' of the countryside, which suggests the clash of values between industrialists and believers in rural traditions.

640 I cannot live with You

In this poem Dickinson offers a closely reasoned argument explaining why she feels forced to renounce her love. It is presented through a speaker, who may be male or female, so the poem is not necessarily autobiographical. This could be a carefully constructed poem of consolation for a love affair that cannot be allowed to develop, in contrast to 322: '*There came a Day at Summer's full*'.

There are six stages to the persuasive argument. In the first, stanzas 1–3, the speaker explains that she is not allowed to lead the life she wants, but is rejected and locked away like a piece of broken china. In stanzas 4 and 5 the argument is about what might happen at death; how could either of the lovers bear to see the other die? Following a logical train of thought, stanzas 6 and 7 consider the idea of resurrection after death; the loved one is thought to be more beautiful than Jesus. As this would be the sin of idolatry, it would not be right to be together after death.

In stanzas 8 and 9 the day of judgement is considered. The loved one tried to observe religious rules, whereas the speaker preferred to look at her lover rather than paradise, again the sin of idolatry. The speaker continues in stanzas 10 and 11 to explain that it would be an impossible situation for both if one were to be saved and went to heaven and the other were condemned to hell; for both, the parting would be unbearable. So having considered natural life and life after death, and having demonstrated the impossibility of being together at any stage, in the last stanza the speaker concludes that the lovers must part. However, it is an odd sort of parting, with the *Door ajar*; it is a half-way measure, balanced between a faint hope and *Despair*. There is no closure.

As in 528: '*Mine – by the Right of the White Election!*' there is a sustained use of religious imagery, secularized for the purposes of the poem. The opening images blend the domestic with the religious, as the wasted life of the lovers is compared to broken china. However, the poet comments that the *Sexton* holds the *Key* to their lives. Perhaps this image suggests that the church would frown on their relationship?

From stanza 6 onwards, religious doctrines are used in what the Puritans would see as blasphemous ways. Jesus's *Grace* and beauty would be outshone by that of the lover; then Dickinson secularizes ideas of heaven and hell. Heaven is the place where the loved one is; hell is the place without him. As in 510: '*It was not Death, for I stood up*', Dickinson plays with images of space in the final stanza; the lovers are only a door's width apart, but they are as far apart as an ocean. Might that suggest that they will be together spiritually and emotionally, but physically apart? The word *Prayer* is ambiguous: will the lovers pray to be together? Or is the notion of prayer as remote to her as the lover is? Again, as in poem 528, the idea of whiteness is used, and could suggest purification; or the negation of all, as the colour white is a negation of all colours. It could be a blasphemous reference to the white communion bread that churchgoers share, whereas these lovers have nothing to sustain them.

Autobiographically, this could be a poem about Dickinson's love for the Reverend Charles Wadsworth, as the church would certainly have forbidden their union. As in 327: '*Before I got my eye put out*' and 528: '*Mine – by the Right of the White Election!*' there might be a literary reference, as it has been suggested that the first line of the poem borrows Cathy's rejection of Heathcliff in Emily Brontë's novel *Wuthering Heights*. In the novel as in the poem religious imagery of heaven and hell are very evident, and Dickinson is known to have admired the writing of the Brontës.

The many dashes in this poem create a sense of agonizing over the decision made, or the situation.

4 **Behind the Shelf** this suggests being locked away, deprived of life. The domestic image of the shelf is developed in lines 7–12 as images of broken china, perhaps suggesting the incompleteness or shattered state of the lovers.
5 The *Sexton* might represent church authority as a whole; he is the warden of a graveyard, so there is also a reference to death.
11 **Sevres** valuable French china.
13 The word *die* might carry sexual connotations, since it is also used to mean achieving a sexual climax, as in John Donne's love poetry.
15 This line suggests the final closing of the eyes after death.
19–20 The *Right of Frost* is a metaphor for the moment of death; for the person dying it is a *privilege* to become numb to events.
21 The word *rise* is related to resurrection.

657 I dwell in Possibility

This is one of Dickinson's poems about her vocation and life as a poet, and is part of the group which includes 327, 441, 709, 741, 1129, and 1138. It is often regarded as an autobiographical poem. It is a visionary poem in which the speaker opens up her spiritual, emotional and intellectual life, inviting the reader to share her viewpoint. Again she uses concrete, physical imagery to present an abstract theme.

In the first stanza the speaker explains why she prefers poetry to prose. The reference to windows and doors might suggest the greater imaginative possibilities. She uses natural imagery in the central stanza to explain that she lives amid the trees and under the stars. This suggests that she lives away from society. The last stanza extends beyond the domestic and natural imagery, as the *Visions* perhaps represent the inspirational thoughts that arrive from time to time. She concludes by suggesting that hers is a vast world of space and imagination, all contained in her *narrow Hands*. The image is a familiar one that Dickinson uses to suggest her relative smallness in comparison with the huge topics she tackles in her poetry.

This poem is compressed and economical, but the ideas suggested are large, and there is play on the concepts of physical space and the space created by the imagination. Dickinson uses the image of windows to suggest the light of day and also the soul or the imagination. Windows allow access to vision, but keep unwanted intruders out; socially, windows in the nineteenth century indicated wealth and status. The poet reverses the idea of social status to stress the intellectual status she feels to be important, and to which she lays claim.

The problem of the limited status of women in nineteenth-century America is addressed by suggesting a withdrawal to the advantageous position of the anonymous prophet/seer observing society safely through windows real and imagined. The poet is thus safe from social pressure, *Impregnable*, and cannot be hurt. However, the word has military connotations of siege warfare, so there is the suggestion that Dickinson has had to battle to achieve this situation. The final word *Paradise* suggests the perfection of her state.

5 **Cedars** large evergreen trees.

8 **Gambrel** an architectural term for the type of roof often built in America where there are two flat surfaces below the apex; it is similar to the roof of a Dutch barn.

663 Again – his voice is at the door

Dickinson plays with perspectives as she uses the time-frame of the present to re-enact a lovers' meeting in the past. Similarly, two states of mind are portrayed as the speaker describes an intense, passionate but forbidden lovers' tryst. The maid asks the gentleman in; the speaker goes to meet him shyly, having picked a flower with which to adorn herself. They confirm the depth of their love and go for a walk beneath the moon. Such was her love that she, the speaker, would die to experience this again, as long as he were there alongside her to count her blood drops as they spilt.

The poem is more of a narrative than a dramatic monologue, but the use of italics makes it a dramatic account and this effect is furthered by the use of dashes to create significant pauses. The poem records two different experiences: the present, with the painful, nostalgic sense of deprivation, and the dramatized and therefore realized account of past passion. The opening word *Again* might suggest that recalling this memory is not unusual; but above all, she deeply desires the meeting to happen all over again. The poem is generally considered to be autobiographical.

The speaker is humble about herself; she feels the *old Degree*, which might imply a degree of emotion, but also the word 'degree' means social status. In stanza 2 she takes a flower to improve her appearance. Perhaps the *mingled steps* suggest an uneven pace as she hesitates. Is she nervous, shy, or is there a decision to be made? What is remarkable about the poem is the lack of close detail: the poet recalls a voice, a flower, a step. Dickinson suggests that this is how memory works; just a few fragments suffice to convey such an intense experience.

The poem continues with the speaker offering further cryptic details such as the way they talk; perhaps words were tossed away along with social convention. Further minute details sketch out the story: the dog left behind (this action emphasizes trust and privacy); and the moon, itself a symbol of romance, but also of Diana the Roman goddess, a symbol of purity. In the last stanza *again* is italicized to make the speaker's feelings clear; to experience this again in reality and not just in memory, the speaker would give her life, as long as he, the loved one, would be there.

Once again religious language is used to convey a human experience. The angels are called as witnesses; the purple in her vein is an echo of Jesus's blood on the cross. Again, for the suffering speaker, human love outshines divine love.

1 The use of common metre in this poem, drawn from church services, perhaps suggests a religious value in the lovers.

8 The exclamation marks throughout the poem dramatize the

emotions of the speaker, helped by the italicizing of the speaker's thoughts.

14 **plummet** suggests talking in low voices.

21–22 The repeated word *alone* suggests that this is the first time that the lovers have been able to meet in this way.

23 This meeting is the first time that they have been able to experience the heavens like *Angels*.

668 'Nature' is what we see

This is another of Dickinson's 'Poems of Definition', in which she attempts to define nature. It may be read in two ways: as being told by a single speaker, who checks herself/himself in the lines beginning *Nay*; or as a dialogue, which might make for a livelier reading.

The poet begins with the sense of sight, suggesting this is how nature is demonstrated. Read as a dialogue, the first speaker defines nature through the senses, and the second in an abstract way. The first voice lists what we see in nature; the second voice refutes this, saying that nature is heaven, the perfection of all things. Then the first voice suggests that nature is what we hear, again to be contradicted by the second voice, who suggests that the hallmark of nature is her harmony. Perhaps both voices are united in perplexity or defeat at lines 9–12. Nature may be intuited, but cannot in its entirety or vastness be explained. Perhaps, the speaker concedes, because our human knowledge and wisdom cannot unravel the simplicity of nature, it is impossible to even attempt to understand her constituent parts.

The speaker goes beyond just listing the various characteristics of nature. At line 8, referring to *Harmony*, perhaps the speaker or poet is implying the perfection in which all aspects are harmonized together. This is a Christian argument for the existence of God made evident in the design of the universe, an argument offered by St Thomas Aquinas. In line 12 the word *Simplicity* could be another reference to this proof of God by design. Dickinson's reading at Mount Holyoke would have included the works of St Thomas Aquinas. There is therefore an implied reference to a Christian belief, but it is impossible to know whether this was intentional, or whether Dickinson herself, as opposed to the speaker, could accept such an argument.

In this view of nature there are Christian overtones and some elements of Romanticism. Dickinson shares the Romantic view of nature as supreme, of great importance to mankind, but in this poem she does not embrace the idea of nature as a teacher. Instead, nature is unknowable. Nor is there a suggestion of a higher, transcendental harmony between man and nature. Nature is omnipotent, all-powerful, but stands as something apart from man. This is one of her most benign accounts of nature, especially when compared with 328: '*A Bird came down the Walk*', 986: '*A narrow Fellow in the Grass*' and 1670: '*In Winter in my Room*'.

6 **Bobolink** an American songbird.

670 One need not be a Chamber – to be Haunted

In this poem the speaker claims that haunted castles and abbeys and even pursuit by an assassin are far less terrifying than a haunted mind, subject to psychological trauma. Once again Dickinson uses elements from the Gothic genre to convey her ideas.

Dickinson bases her extended comparisons or analogies once again on a series of opposed situations. The first metaphor compares the chamber of a haunted house to the *Brain* as a dwelling place with its *Corridors*. The haunting of a castle is compared to the haunting of a mind by trauma. The poet tries to establish just how terrifying mental problems can be. It is possible to flee from an abbey ghost because such hauntings are well known, so the visitor is prepared. In the case of *lonesome* conflict, one cannot flee. Likewise it is possible to flee from a would-be murderer (stanza 4), so that particular danger would be less horrific than having to face a disturbed mind. The last stanza uses irony to emphasize how unprepared a person is for psychological problems. Whatever the person does for self-protection, such as *bolts the Door*, defences are useless.

As in 280: *'I felt a Funeral, in my Brain'* and 465: *'I heard a Fly buzz – when I died'*, the Gothic effects are obvious; there are haunted castles and abbeys; threats of murder; an isolated, helpless victim. All of these stock devices are chilling and effectively portray a highly disturbed state of mind. Again, Dickinson has presented an abstract idea with concrete examples. The rhyme scheme matches the moods by varying between half and full rhymes. The final masculine rhyme on *Door/More* enacts a sense of a door slamming shut and being bolted, but the incomplete last line and the final dash deny closure. Perhaps this might suggest that further developments are too horrid to contemplate. Behind the voice of the speaker could well be that of Dickinson herself, as she endured agonizing traumas; this poem could well have autobiographical roots.

3–4 **surpassing/Material Place** unseen, abstract mental haunting is worse than that of an actual place.

8 **Cooler Host** the rational mind, as opposed to a heated imagination.

690 Victory comes late

This poem is written very much in the mood and tone of 67: *'Success is counted sweetest'* and 444: *'It feels a shame to be Alive'*, but Dickinson goes much further here in having the speaker attack God for his failure to care for man. It is suggested that God is negligent, uncaring, mean-spirited and cruel – assuming he is there at all!

War would be tolerable if it were seen to be part of a divine plan for the improvement of mankind. The trouble was that there was no evidence of such a plan, and the Civil War was tearing families and the nation apart, wrecking the old order which Dickinson loved. The question considered in the poem is how God can be indifferent to the sufferings of mankind. Dickinson wrote to her cousins that she 'sang off charnel steps'; in other words she wrote poems such as this metaphorically standing on the edge of the battlefield, with her thoughts immersed in the subject of war.

The speaker asks what the point of victory is when it comes too late for the dead and for the dying. Victory is described as drink or nourishment offered to someone too advanced in the process of dying.

God is *economical*, a word with a financial register appropriate to a society based solely on economics and commerce, which is how Dickinson sees nineteenth-century America. The community has gained power from war, and power means money.

In the last five lines the image becomes that of a bird table at which symbolic birds are denied food until they starve. God is denying those who are most dependent on him. There is an ironic echo of the lines of Psalm 23: 'Thou preparest a table before me in the presence of mine enemies;... my cup runneth over'.

The ideas of the individual and the community could be represented by the sparrow and the robin respectively (elsewhere Dickinson has used the robin to represent New England); the eagle is also the emblem of the United States. On this reading, God has denied all three levels of human community; the eagle (US), the robin (New England) and the sparrow (the individual). The use of the image of the sparrow is important. In the Sermon on the Mount, Jesus said that if 'the least sparrow should fall to earth', God would be aware of him. This is horribly reversed in this poem, as the sparrow is left to die. The *Golden Breakfast* (to be shared with God on our resurrection), and the golden vision of the Pilgrim fathers on which so much faith was based, are seen to have vanished; the eagle chokes on what has been fed to him.

The free verse form, unusual for Dickinson, supports the sense of chaos and disorder in the poem. The final dash might suggest ongoing despair and no hope of future closure. The poem stands as an elegy for all lost in war, and for the loss of social order and of faith.

709 Publication – is the Auction

This poem is linked to 303: '*The Soul selects her own Society*', 528: '*Mine – by the Right of the White Election!*' and 657: '*I dwell in Possibility*'. It is a disputation about writing poetry, personal values and the dangers of commercialism. It is probably autobiographical, the exploration or justification of Dickinson's decisions about allowing her poetry to enter the public arena. She was acutely aware of the burden of social expectations that women must be supportive of a husband, quiet, passive and retiring. To write for money was to go against the grain of 'normal' female behaviour, unless financial circumstances made this necessary.

The poet attacks the idea of putting a price on her poetry, to sell it like a *Parcel* (13), reducing the poet's precious and divine gift to a mere commodity. In contrast to this, Dickinson offers the vision of the poet in isolation in the *Garret* (6), pure in spirit and pure in mind, as the whiteness might suggest, maintaining a spiritual pact with God who gave this talent to the poet. She sees it as a *Disgrace* (16), to reduce the human spirit to cash dealings.

There are two levels of imagery in the poem. There is the image of female prostitution, *We* representing women as well as poets. The words *White* (7) and *Snow* (8) suggest the purity which must not be soiled by selling to the merchant. At the second level there is the poet, the *Mind of Man* (2), suggesting at first the male gender of so many of the great poets. Should the poet sell off the products of God's gifts? *Corporeal illustration* (11) is a compressed image: the word *Corporeal* means 'of the body', so it could suggest the *Thought* of the poem made flesh by or in the poet; and also the image of the prostitute selling her body, merged with the image of selling poetry to a publisher.

Dickinson uses images of the white purity of the artist set in opposition to images of commercialism. There is accordingly a contrast of register between the words relating to the artist in the *Garret* such as *White* and *Snow*, and the register of commerce and merchandising, such as *Sell*, *Merchant* and *Price*. The question of whether to sell her poetry for a price is connected to all of her concerns about how to maintain her integrity and keep her identity in an age where everything, even human endeavour and human life, was viewed in cash terms.

The poem bears witness to Dickinson's decision not to put her poems into print. About 12 were published in her lifetime in *The Springfield Observer*; at least 500 were sent to friends and family, and the majority was sewn into 'fascicles' discovered by her sister Lavinia after her death. The poem also bears witness to her decision to retire to her bedroom and to wear white, the symbol of purity, innocence, and lack of gender.

1 The dashes throughout the poem suggest the density of the thought, marking its development. The final dash leaves the poem open, as the debate is unfinished personally, socially and historically.

12 **Royal Air** a song inspired by God, the king of heaven, as opposed to earth and earthly matters.

13 **Parcel** a technical term for goods or land sold at auction; it is also a package sent through the post for which money has been paid.

712 Because I could not stop for Death

This dramatic monologue is an extended metaphor in which a lady appears to describe a pleasant evening drive with a courteous, gallant gentleman. The reader realizes that this is in fact an account of the journey through life to death, and possibly eternity. The first line of the poem is quite shocking, but the tone is relaxed and calm, established by the use of the adverbs *kindly* and *slowly*. The lady is clearly polite and responds to the courteous attentions of the gentleman; there is almost an erotic edge to the poem, which is typical of Romantic views of death. The gentleman could be the equivalent of the ferryman of ancient Greek literature, who rowed heroes to their final rest.

Dickinson presents life as an unavoidable journey towards death and eternity; again she uses contrasts to help develop her themes. The carriage has a rather spooky, unseen third passenger, *Immortality*. The speaker surveys, apparently in a carefree way, the various stages of life in a rural society. These images represent the various stages of human life: childhood, with the vision of the school; maturity, with the image of the ripening harvest; and death approaching as the setting sun. All of these are Romantic images, serving similar purposes as they did for John Keats in his Odes. Dickinson was known to be fond of Keats's poetry.

There is a change in the second half of the poem; the speaker corrects herself in line 13, and admits that as soon she realized that they were heading for eternity, she had no choice but to accept this fate.

The common metre is reversed in lines 13–14, perhaps to mark this change, although the alliteration on the hushed 's' and quiet 't' sounds remains unchanged. The speaker's vulnerability is stressed as her clothes seem too light for the cold evening journey: might they be burial clothes? Might the chill be that of approaching death? The speaker uses familiar domestic imagery, the *Roof* and the *Cornice* (19 and 20), which seems chilling here because the usual reassuring associations are reversed and they become symbols of the grave.

But the journey doesn't stop there; they proceed to *Eternity*. There is the usual ambiguity: they are heading towards *Eternity*, but do they or will they ever reach it? The reader doesn't know, and this uncertainty is sustained at the end of the poem by the use of the dash and consequent lack of closure. Yet again, Dickinson refuses to declare a belief in resurrection; the only certainty is death as a deprivation of life, which is made clear in stanza 3.

As in 216: *'Safe in their Alabaster Chambers'*, the poet plays with time and space. The reader has no idea whether *Eternity* is ever reached, or where the speaker is now, or even when this occurred; it was *Centuries* ago. From this vast perspective the repeated story of a human life seems insignificant; and this sense is deepened as there is no hint of anything to hope for after death, despite the ghostly presence of *Immortality* in the carriage.

Several readings have been suggested for this poem, often relying on the poet's use of the present tense *feels* in the last stanza. Is this simply the voice of the speaker looking back posthumously? Might it be a dramatization of the poet's sudden awareness of the unchanging conditions of her life, and her rejection of ordinary activities and beliefs? Could Dickinson be presenting herself as a corpse, a ghost in society, or might she be reminiscing about a 'fatal' love affair? Perhaps there is something of all these meanings in the poem.

9–12 The repetition (or anaphora) of *passed* in stanza 3 enforces the idea of the finality of the journey, as these 'markers' or stages are left behind.

10 Perhaps the *Ring* is a reminder of childhood games, but also of the journey through life as a circle: we end where we began.

14 The alliteration on 'd' and the use of the near-homonyms *Dews* and *drew* might suggest life slowing down for death as the pace of the poem seems to slow.

15 **Gossamer** a delicate, almost transparent fabric. *Tulle* in the following line is also a delicate fabric. These two fabrics might suggest the frailty of humanity.

16 **Tippet** a little cape.

20 **Cornice** an architectural term for moulding on a ceiling or roof.

732 She rose to His Requirement – dropt

Dickinson here addresses a woman's choice of marriage, as she gives up the freedom and pleasures of youth and faces up to her new status as a wife. It is a poem about identity and selfhood.

Dickinson again uses contrast to develop her ideas, but it is uncertain whether any judgement on marriage is made. The use of contrast immediately creates a double movement in the first line of the poem: she *rose* as a wife, but *dropt* her girlhood past. Is this an improvement for the woman? The contrast between the light of *Her new Day* (5), and the darkness of the deep *Fathoms* (12), again raises questions about her choice, but these are not articulated fully. Is the contrast made between *honorable* (3) and *Playthings* (2) designed to elevate a wife's role in marriage? Or is it used ironically to suggest a life of sacrifice to *His Requirement*, perhaps capitalized for stress?

What might be implied about the contrast between the woman's previous life, with its *Amplitude*, *Awe*, *first Prospective*, and her subsequent life as a married woman with the *Gold* now wearing away? Do these words suggest enrichment or impoverishment? What is made clear is that the woman is deliberately keeping this to herself: *It lay unmentioned* (9), and in a way Dickinson is writing in the same way: she expresses no clear view. The author seems to leave it open-ended, as if no one knows what goes on in the mind of a married woman. However, if a wife keeps all to herself, what is her emotional and spiritual state?

The metaphor of the sea is often used to suggest a spiritual state, but Dickinson also uses images of *Pearl* and *Weed* (10). Perhaps these might be used to represent spiritual values. Does the *Weed* overcome the *Pearl*, suggesting that marriage chokes and darkens a woman's life? Or are the words to be held as equal in value as natural developments in married life? Does the *Weed* suggest natural and healthy growth in which the woman will be happy, or the opposite? Have the feelings, emotions and spiritual values of the married woman been weakened or strengthened? It is all unclear in this poem. Again, Dickinson has used natural and concrete examples to define a mental state, but this remains ambiguous.

The *Himself* (11), who understands the *Fathoms* or depths of this relationship, could be the husband, capitalized as in the first line. Or it might be *the Sea* (9), perhaps an image of Neptune or of the Old Man of the Sea. Or might it be God, who ordained marriage as a sacrament? Dickinson has offered clues to a psychological state, without revealing her views. The final choice of reading(s) rests with the individual reader.

1 The word *dropt* is pointedly placed as the last word of the line to draw attention to the contrast with *rose*. A dash has been used to create the pause which emphasizes this juxtaposition.

12 **Fathom** a traditional measurement of the depth of the sea.

741 Drama's Vitallest Expression is the Common Day

This poem is significant in helping to define Dickinson's views on human life and on the role of the poet. It is a poem about defining identity and selfhood. Essentially she focuses on the sheer drama of human existence, presented as a series of performances (indicated by the word *Recitation* in line 4) or dramas (such as *Hamlet* in line 8) where a wide range of human experiences are presented. Life is often tragic; and the struggle not to *Perish* (4) is as significant in everyday life as any drama to be seen on stage. The business of life is seen to be the most important matter for literature.

Throughout the poem she again uses oppositions, this time between real life and presentations on stage. It is outside of the theatre where the real dramas happen. The greatest drama is enacted in the emotions of the human heart, which is the only theatre that cannot be closed by its owner – the person to whom the heart belongs.

The poem links with 657: *'I dwell in Possibility'*, for example, in presenting thoughts about writing poetry. It is similar to 446: *'I showed her Heights she never saw'*, where the speaker projects a male personality, as the conventions of this poem suggest maleness in the reference to the male writer, to a male tragic hero, and to theatre owners, who were usually male in that period. Dickinson makes scholarly references to tragedy, suggesting that she writes for an educated readership who would understand the choices offered in this poem: either take life on with its drama, or sit it out as a spectator. The use of *Us* in the first stanza might suggest that the poet's challenge will be taken up by the reader.

12–15 The last stanza stands alone as an aphorism – a persuasive statement which sounds authoritative. The human heart is the theatre, and the individual is the theatre owner. This idea of ownership might imply a responsibility to face up to the drama of life; by surviving, to keep it going. To fail to do so would be to neglect one's duties, just as there would be a failure if a production were to falter.

747 It dropped so low – in my Regard

This poem is linked to 213: *'Did the Harebell loose her girdle'*, as the speaker initially considers whether the value of something once it has been achieved is lower than when it seemed to be inaccessible. There is no clarification of what *It* is; again, in the metaphor of pottery Dickinson uses a concrete example to define a state of mind, and again she uses opposites. The first stanza is used to describe *It* failing, with the metaphor of pottery shattering on the floor. The poet makes sure the reader understands the point by making *in my Regard* an aside from the speaker to the reader, indicated by the use of dashes. This is a poem concerned entirely with the speaker's view and the quality of his or her judgement.

The second stanza makes the problem clearer and brings in a note of regret, perhaps over an error of judgement. Initially the speaker tried to blame something or someone else, *the Fate that flung it* (5), but finally has to take the responsibility for over-valuing it. The use of the image of the *Plated* ware compared to *Silver* makes this clear. The poem ends by the speaker admitting to bad judgement, perhaps provoking the reader into some self-analysis. The poem might be autobiographical, and because of the use of the domestic imagery of the shelf and the pottery, plated ware and silverware, the speaker is most likely female. Whether the speaker is the poet remains unclear.

2/4 The use of masculine half-rhyme (*Ground/Mind*) might suggest a firm voice.

3 **Stones** might suggest a tiled kitchen floor, as well as the ground outside.

7 **Plated Wares** vessels made of a common, inexpensive material such as copper, and plated to look as if made of silver or gold.

8 **Silver Shelf** the shelf where the housewife keeps her most expensive trinkets and plates.

754 My Life had stood – a Loaded Gun

This is perhaps the most startling first line of all in Dickinson's poems, immediately establishing the metaphor in which a loaded gun is used to represent the speaker's life, or certain aspects of the speaker's life. The metaphor is sustained throughout the poem, which presents a day's hunting after the owner identifies and picks up his gun. At night the gun guards its *Master* and is deadly to his enemies. The curious last stanza is cryptic: although *I*, the speaker, cannot die, the Master must live longer.

The tone of the poem suggests the pleasure of hunting, emphasized by the anaphora of *And* (stanza 2). There is a sense of the power of the weapon as the crack of the rifle forces nature, the mountains, to respond. The senses are developed from sound to sight as the flash of the bullet firing is recorded as *cordial* (9). A cordial was originally a tonic for the heart, the exact opposite of the purpose of a bullet. Despite the presentation, the reader is reminded that the gun is deadly, almost as if it has a will of its own.

In stanza 4 there is a suggestion of choice, as the gun prefers to guard the Master's bed, than to sleep alongside him on his pillow. The deadliness of the gun is enforced in the fifth stanza with the reference to the *Yellow Eye*. This probably relates the flash of gunpowder to the yellow eye of a snake, often seen as a symbol of evil.

Much of this poem supports a Gothic reading; there is death, suspense, waiting and watching, and a female victim (6). The *Yellow Eye* recalls the eyes Frankenstein noted when his creature came to life. Could it be that the reference to *Master* also echoes the creature addressing Frankenstein? Might there be a suggestion that in designing and using the gun, mankind has made its own monster? Dickinson had read *Frankenstein*, and such a reading would support her anti-war views. Perhaps Dickinson is allowing the gun to speak for itself about the catastrophe of weaponry and war, which, as the final dash might suggest, is ongoing. Such a reading might be supported by the fact that that the representative of natural and healthy female life, *the Doe*, is killed. The implication would be that life has now become too masculinized and too destructive.

There are many other possible readings. There are echoes of life on the American frontier, possibly inverted to become the words of a female adventurer. There is a suggestion of femininity in the domestic detail of the bed, and Dickinson often used the volcano as an image of the inner strength of women (11). Or could it be that the gun is an image of poetry, with the bullets representing words? Truly, words do have the power to kill, and outlive their creator. If the power of the 'Master/poet' is to be sustained, if this 'gun' is to be used to full purpose as the poetic gift, then he or she must continue to live. He or she is human and cannot live for ever, but words live on. Such a reading would resolve the riddle of the last stanza.

Other readers suggest that the poem might be about love and the power of love. By being identified and selected by a *Master*, the woman would be empowered as she grew in identity in her love relationship. Or perhaps the poem might be about God as the Master, with his *emphatic Thumb*; this might refer not only to the pulling of the trigger, but to his power over life and death, just as Roman emperors used their thumbs to indicate whether a gladiator were to live or to die. To a believer, this poem might suggest the impossibility of achieving free will independent of God. God will always pull the trigger to determine our actions. Finally, there is an echo of the ongoing Civil War. Of course all of these meanings, and more, could co-exist.

5 **Sovereign** a tribute to the greatness of nature.
9 **cordial** used ambiguously; both life-giving and life-threatening.
11 Vesuvius is a volcanic mountain in southern Italy; Dickinson often used this as a symbol of the hidden power of women.
13 The phrase *Our good Day done* and the reference to guarding has echoes of the night prayer said before sleep; again there is secularization of religious language.
15 an *Eider-Duck* has very soft feathers used for filling pillows.

986 A narrow Fellow in the Grass

In this poem the male speaker describes a snake in the grass, as if to a young child, including how it looks, how it moves and where it lives. After the speaker's description of a boyhood incident, the tone of the poem changes and it ends on a darker note about the fear this creature can induce.

The tone is playful at first and the New England accent would have made a comic internal rhyme on *narrow Fellow* (1). The poem initially has the form of a riddle as the word 'snake' is avoided, and the reader has to guess what the subject matter is. The rhythm of the first two stanzas is that of common metre, and the combination of an eight-syllable line followed by a six-syllable line perhaps mimics the snake's coiling and uncoiling as it moves. Throughout these two stanzas there is alliteration on the soft 's' sound, which suggests the sound of the snake hissing.

The visual imagery is developed in the simile of the comb parting grass (5), which is immediately qualified by the word *shaft* (6), introducing a metaphor for the snake's body and head. It is a rather sinister picture of the grass silently parting and closing; is this the first hint of something darker in the poem? Dickinson's knowledge of nature is evident in the description of the habitat; but the reader notes that this is *Boggy* and *too cool* (9–10) for the harvest which supports life for both animals and humans; already the snake is seen to be alien to mankind. In the long middle stanza the rhythm changes and the use of dashes helps to introduce a more conversational tone. Here the snake is described as a *Whip lash* (13), which increases the sense of alienation from the animal world.

The speaker explains that generally he feels cordial towards *Nature's People* (17); the phrase indicates a respect for nature and is also playful. Dickinson uses contrast to make a major point in the last stanza, however. The snake seems terrifying as the speaker gasps for breath and feels the extreme chill of fear.

In biblical imagery, the snake is always linked to evil. After its appearance in the Garden of Eden, a snake destroyed human innocence and joy. Perhaps, therefore, the poem might have a wider meaning, suggesting that in life there is always danger – the snake in the grass – so we must be on our guard. Perhaps the poem is something of a moral fable?

11 The capitalized *Boy* and *Barefoot* stress the innocence and ignorance of the youngster walking unwittingly into danger.

19/20 The phrase a *transport/Of cordiality* introduces a comic tone; perhaps this is used to contrast to the note of terror at the end of the poem.

24 **Zero at the Bone** a solemn-sounding phrase with a deep 'o' sound; and with the full masculine rhyme with *alone*, it sounds final, perhaps to suggest the finality of a dangerous snake-bite.

1068 Further in Summer than the Birds

This poem resembles 258: '*There's a certain Slant of light*', where a particular trick of light leads to meditation. Here, the chorus of grasshoppers, crickets and such insects in the grass leads to a meditation about the end of summer, with the tone at the end of the poem projecting a sombre mood. Again the poet uses religious language and applies it to nature to create a ceremonial and ritualistic effect. Religious references abound, such as *Mass* (4), *Ordinance* (5) and *Canticle* (11). These are combined with many visual and aural images of nature.

In stanza 1 a *minor Nation*, the miniature insect world, is celebrating its customary ritual of late summer. The opening phrase *Further in Summer* is rather obscure. The word *Further* might suggest that the insect ceremony is later in summer than when the birds are busy. It might suggest that this ceremony is more significant to summer than the birds themselves are.

The insects are described as *Pathetic* (2), such pathos linking to the general chastened mood of the poem; the word might also suggest that they are sympathetic to the rites of nature and also to the mood of the speaker/observer. The poem opens with the sense of sight, and the words *minor* and *Mass* bring in the aural sense. A mass sung in a minor key would probably be sad and solemn. The word *celebrates* (3) links the religious and natural imagery together.

In stanza 2 the speaker explains that although no religious

rites are seen, a sense, like *Grace*, pervades the listener, who begins to feel thoughtful.

In stanza 3 the insects sing a *spectral* or ghostly hymn. The word *Antiquest* (9) is an unusual use of the superlative which makes a reader pause momentarily; linked to the world of the Druids (15), there is an emphasis on how old this custom is. Perhaps there is also a sense of an 'anti-quest' or reverse quest; searching in nature for an understanding about human life, the observer instead discovers thoughts about death, so the purpose of the quest is reversed.

Ironically there is the contrast here between the burning August heat and the ghostly presence of the creatures; even at this time of high summer, life and death are inter-connected. The last line of this stanza, *Repose to typify*, is ambiguous; this disturbing thought may reflect what happens when the poet's mind tries to seek rest; or perhaps this sacramental activity is typical of the prelude to death, or *Repose* as it is for the insects.

The final stanza enforces this mood of thoughtfulness. The *Canticle* (11) introduced a mood of pathos, disquiet, or solemnity. Although summer has lost none of her grace, and there is no visual evidence that summer will fade, this solemn ritual has served its purpose. Nature, as old as the Druid religion, but also like the Druids unknowable, and impassive like their monuments, has changed. The speaker feels saddened at this experience. The shock was the glimpse of mutability. All things must change; change must eventually bring decay for all things natural and human. The ceremony of the insects has become a requiem mass, a mass for the dead.

3 The phrase *A minor Nation* suggests the smallness of the insects, and how insignificant they are compared to man, yet to themselves they are a nation.

4 **Mass** an important church service. There is also a reference to the vast number of these insects.

5 **Ordinance** a religious rite.

11 **spectral** ghostly.

Canticle a little hymn sung out of a prayer book.

14 The phrase *Furrow on the Glow* merges the senses of sight and touch, with the reference to a furrow ploughed into the glowing face of nature.

1072 Title divine – is mine!

As with 690: '*Victory comes late*', this poem stands at a crossroads in Dickinson's poetry; it draws in all of her major concerns, love, war, poetry, problems in society, problems about belief in God. All of these issues work together as she vows to use her art of poetry as her support. Most readers see this as an autobiographical poem, as Dickinson describes the state in which she lives.

Title divine opens the poem on a note of ambiguity, which is its hallmark. The precise meaning of the poem is uncertain. The speaker claims that she is a wife *without the Sign* (2), and not just an ordinary wife. Then she claims to be the *Empress of Calvary* (4), which suggests that she is suffering, but that it is a noble suffering, perhaps out of choice. Some readers see this as a reference to the Reverend Charles Wadsworth, who had to leave for Calvary church, San Francisco, to work in a new parish, leaving her to suffer alone. The wife is both empowered but also disempowered and dispossessed. (His absence would explain this.) The wife is *Royal* (5), but does not have visible insignias; she is *Betrothed* (engaged), but not in the traditionally romantic way.

The first lines with the use of the dashes and exclamation marks seem positive and excited. Perhaps the title is *divine* not simply because God created the sacrament of marriage, but in another reading because the title may refer to poetry, and the chosen title of poet may be seen as a divine gift, and something better than most women desire or expect. Also, unlike the average woman, the speaker will be acclaimed for her poetry after her death, as Jesus was acclaimed after his resurrection.

Interestingly the speaker identifies God as the source of

women's tendency to faint (6–7). The phrase *Garnet to Garnet* (8) has many connotations: of garnet wedding rings; of the red blood of passion when two hearts meet; of the red blood shed on Calvary in the crucifixion. However, as this is a gemstone, the speaker is perhaps making a reference to social customs and expectations.

Perhaps there is irony in the account of the woman swooning – a mockery of sentimentality. However, lines 10 and 11 are devastating: *Born – Bridalled – Shrouded –/In a Day –*. This image reveals Dickinson's scornful assessment of marriage. A woman on her wedding day is *Born* as a wife, but also will have much to 'bear' or endure; she is *Bridalled*, celebrating her wedding day, but also there is a sense of being controlled and perhaps broken, as a pony may be put into a bridle; and the wedding veil is also like a shroud, symbolizing the death of a woman's independence as in 732: '*She rose to His Requirement – dropt*'. Conventional marriage is seen as a triple victory for men (12). At this point it becomes clear that as *Empress of Calvary*, the speaker might suffer, but she is better off than most women; she has made her choice and directed her own future as a poet.

The last three lines are puzzling. Are they meant as a mockery of women who are proud to use this title as a sign of their status, creating marital harmony, a *Melody* (14) for two, or might Dickinson be one of these women, but with a different husband, a different master to serve? The last two lines are erotic if read as referring to sexual pleasures, rather like the idea of *Rowing in Eden* in 249: '*Wild Nights – Wild Nights!*'. These lines might also refer to the music of poetry, and the delicate 'stroke' which makes poetry musical and pleasurable – and perhaps somewhat erotic in the pleasure given to the writer. The last line may be the flirting of a wife. On the other hand it might be the speaker or Dickinson asking the reader if she, the writer, has the rhythms and music of the poetry right. In both cases the tone of coquettishness or shyness would be appropriate.

Does Dickinson finally link herself to all women through a similar experience, or does she remain apart? Readers sometimes see this as a love poem, recalling the joys and suffering of marriage. Others see it as an open attack on conventional marriage and attitudes in what the poet might regard as the battle of the sexes. However, many readers feel that Dickinson is talking about the power of art, specifically poetry, and a complete sense of vocation; here an erotic frisson is not out of place.

1–2 The dashes create a pause to stress the importance of the last phrase in each line; the exclamation marks show the speaker's excitement and delight. The use of full rhyme makes for a confident start to the poem.

3 The phrase *Acute Degree* suggests a title of high status, but also has a sense of wisdom, of being 'acute' in making an astute choice.

4 **Calvary** the hill where Jesus was crucified.

13/15 The restoration of full masculine rhyme seems to end the poem on a confident note.

15 The word *this* might be italicized to suggest the voice of the woman as she asks a question of her husband, or might point to this particular poem to ask a question of the reader.

1100 The last Night that She lived

In poem 465: *'I heard a Fly buzz – when I died'*, Dickinson presented the death of a woman through the woman's own eyes partly as a Gothic experience, secularized and without any thoughts of resurrection. Once again in this poem a woman dies, but here the viewpoint is focused on a group of watchers who share the experience, and the presentation is detached and non-dramatic. It feels as though rigid control is imposed over the feelings. The actual death is recorded in a brief and unremarkable way; the death was almost casual, with no real struggle.

The tone is low-key and again secularized. The poem begins by plunging straight into the business of the dying. Again Dickinson uses contrast to show the difference between the busyness of the watchers and the accepting stillness of the dying woman. Throughout, the emphasis is on the effects of the dying on the watchers; ordinary things seem remarkable now. Then they feel angry, and too disturbed to speak.

But suddenly perspective changes as the woman dies. Dickinson again uses synecdoche to establish the experience, as the woman becomes reduced to only the *Hair*, then just a *Head*; full human status has disappeared as death crept over her. The use of the definite article 'the', instead of 'her', implies that now the woman has lost her gender and her individuality.

There is a sense of feelings being controlled in the repetition of *We* (25); this perhaps suggests a sob. Perhaps the watchers are thinking about how to control or *regulate* (28) their feelings, so that they conform to convention.

Dickinson had seen her invalided mother die, and perhaps her experience comes through in this poem. Death is seen as something natural; the woman dies *lightly as a Reed* which *Bent to the Water* (22–23). No supernatural element is suggested, and there is no reference to God or resurrection; death seems final. Significantly, the *awful* aspect of the death is that the watchers now have nothing left to do but face up to the fact that the woman has died. At one time, when religious belief was strong, there would have been awe at the thought of facing the majesty of Jesus Christ after death. Also, it is possible that the words *Belief to regulate* suggest that the watchers must pay lip service to conventional beliefs about death and resurrection.

18 The word *narrow* is often used by Dickinson as a kind of shorthand. Here perhaps it reflects the way the watchers had to constrain their strong emotions.

1129 Tell all the Truth but tell it slant

This poem reads in a natural way, as though the speaker is letting the reader into professional secrets, and may be linked to poems such as 657: '*I dwell in Possibility*' and 1286: '*I thought that nature was enough'*. The opening line explains the proposition that it is better to soften ideas. In the rest of the poem the speaker offers three reasons or examples: first that the light of truth is too *bright* (3) for human eyes; second that lightning is less frightening to children when it has been kindly explained; and third, the writer returns to the image of revealed truths being so *bright* that they will *dazzle* and *blind* the viewer/reader.

The language used reveals much about Dickinson's views on the role of the poet as prophet or visionary, along the lines of 657: *'I dwell in Possibility'*. There is no doubt about the wisdom and rightness of the poet, or the significance of the role; the poet can reveal eternal truths. There is a gentle pun on the word *slant*, as in America this is a term for half-rhyme; half-rhyme gives the impression of a rhyme, but is not a true one. This implies that something appearing to be the truth should be told, but not the full truth.

The second line sounds like an aphorism, emphasized by the alliteration of 's'. The tone is confident and informed. The alliteration of *superb surprise* (4) might be seen to emphasize the idea of the undoubted importance of what the poet has to say.

Two images in the second stanza, *Lightning* and then blindness, might suggest that the readers are like *Children*, who need to be taught carefully. These images might also suggest the frailty of human reason and emotion, which could be damaged by too direct an address. Perhaps this sounds arrogant, but Dickinson does use the word *our* (3), linking herself to the reader and suggesting that she too has had to struggle to absorb this fact.

The poem, written in regular common metre, reads as a hymn to the seriousness of poetry and to the importance of the role of its authors. The final dash, denying closure, might suggest that both poet and reader may benefit if they persist in their respective roles in the pursuit of truth.

1138 A Spider sewed at Night

In this extremely abstract poem, Dickinson works through a complex metaphor comparing the spider spinning its web to the poet creating poetry. As with the speakers of many of the dramatic monologues, Dickinson presents the spider as male; he spins alone at night, making a web entirely of his own design and for his own purposes. This could be a re-working of an earlier poem that she could not finish; here she does succeed in drawing the *Physiognomy*, perhaps the profile, of her poetry.

In the first stanza the isolation of the poet is stressed; it is night, and there is no light. The *Arc of White* (3) might suggest the blank page the poet faces, or the white might be a suggestion of eternity.

In the second stanza there are two suggestions. The poet/spider will speak in universal terms of matters of life (the *Ruff… of Dame* (4)) and death (the *Shroud of Gnome* (5)); he will keep specific details to himself, and he will freely select his own suject matter.

In the first two stanzas Dickinson has perhaps established the *Physiognomy* of her writing: it must be eternal, and not tied down to any particular time or place. The riddling third stanza sums up all of this. It might be easier to deconstruct this stanza if we read first line 2, then line 1, and then line 3. The aim of the spider/poet as creator was to achieve a certain type of work that was to be immortal. The quiet 's' alliteration throughout the poem suggests thoughtfulness and certainty.

With references to the spider sewing/spinning, Dickinson is drawing on myth by suggesting a link to the ancient Greek Fates, who wove the patterns of human history. The references to the darkness, *Shroud*, and *Gnome* also carry echoes of the more modern Gothic tradition. Perhaps Dickinson is writing her own myth or legend about great poets.

There can also be a darker reading of a terrifying vision presented in this poem. The spider is male; he works in the dark, which implies that he is invisible and unknowable. In spinning the ruffs of dames, perhaps he is responsible for certain aspects of society. In weaving the shrouds of gnomes, does the spider deal out death, and bring evils to the world? Could this dreadful spider represent the uncaring God whom Dickinson criticizes so harshly? Might the *Physiognomy* refer to God-made-flesh in the form of Jesus, who like God the father is immortal? It is a bleak concept.

1183 Step lightly on this narrow spot

This delicate war poem has such wide implications that it stands at the intersection of all Dickinson's concerns for both herself as a poet, and for poetry as a whole. The poem reflects the background of the recent Civil War, as Dickinson contemplates the buried soldier-hero.

In the first stanza the poet seems to address the reader, describing the grave and commenting that the *Breast*, or heart/courage, of the soldier buried there was wider than any land on earth. The second stanza brings in the idea of poetry and the poet. The reader (and perhaps the hero himself) can walk tall; for as long as there are nations and warfare, his name will be known. In the penultimate line the word *Fame* introduces the notion of the poet, whose role is to broadcast this news in the eternal lines of poetry.

The relationship between the individual and the state is touched on in the first stanza. The soldier has a *narrow* grave, but his heart is ample. It is possible that Dickinson is suggesting here the dependence of even the largest nation on each individual, illustrated in this sacrificial death. The state must respect this sacrifice. The anaphora of *Step* and the similarity of sound in each stanza between *lightly* and *lofty* reinforce them as instructions, although the tone is quiet.

In the second stanza it is made clear that this was a death in war; the *Cannon* and *Flag* are metonyms for arms and the army or nation. Dickinson is aware of her role as a poet to present the *deathless Syllable*; through poetry, such *Fame* will survive.

This poem is unfaltering in the use of common metre, the rhythm of hymns, which seems well suited to the subject matter. The alliteration on the quiet 's' and liquid 'l' sounds, and the use of feminine and half-rhyme, maintain a softened tone. This poem links together Dickinson's views on society, on man's responsibility to the state and vice versa, on love and respect, on war and on the role of the poet. Again, there is no suggestion of a redemptive scheme of history in which war plays a part. Eternal life will be gained through poetry.

4 **Emerald Seams** these might represent the seams of the uniform, now mossy or mildewed; the green outline of the grave; and the poet's own seams, which formed the fascicles for her poetry.

1263 There is no Frigate like a Book

In this light-hearted poem, Dickinson suggests the magic and power of reading, especially the reading of poetry. The speaker works through a series of images which portray this magic. The central metaphor rests on the way that poetry 'transports' us. The first image is that of the *Frigate*, or ship, which takes the traveller to different lands; a frigate is also a tropical bird. It is suggested that poetry will take the reader into a new world, and the image of the bird perhaps supports the speed and the naturalness with which this movement can be made.

The speaker goes on to claim that the delightful effects of poetry work more speedily than the fastest horse, or *Courser*, could carry us. Reading poetry is then compared to travelling a road where no toll is charged; it costs little to nourish the soul. The final image is that of the *Chariot* carrying the soul to a higher plane. The overall meaning is that it costs little time or effort to be transported by the power of poetry to higher and more nourishing experiences.

The poem is presented as a complete thought; the dashes indicate the thought in process and this is completed by the final full stop. The rhyme in the explanatory lines 2 and 4, *away/Poetry*, is a feminine half-rhyme indicating incompleteness, whereas the full masculine rhyme at the end, *Toll/soul*, supports the notion of a completed thought. The alliterative 'p' sounds in lines 3 and 4 yield to the sombre and elevated register of the last two lines. Perhaps there is an echo of the Negro spiritual *Swing low, sweet chariot*, which certainly Dickinson would have known. The chariot takes the soul to heaven, and metaphorically poetry can do this.

1 **Frigate** a fast cruiser or warship; also the name of a tropical bird.
3 **Courser** a swift horse.
5 **Traverse** to cross, and in mountaineering a tricky climb across a mountain face.
7 **frugal** to be very careful in spending.

1286 I thought that nature was enough

In this poem the role of the poet is considered, along with his/her relationship to fellow human beings, to nature and to the divine. In the first stanza the proposition is explained; for a time the speaker thought that nature was all that was needed for contemplation, but came to realize that considerations of human nature overshadowed those of general nature. The image of the parallax is used to make this clear. From certain perspectives the flame of a candle seems to disappear, or merge into the body of the candle; in the same way, thoughts of mankind seem to eliminate thoughts about nature.

There is ambiguity in the second stanza. Perhaps it is suggested that through awareness of human nature, thoughts of God will inevitably arise. The speaker in this reading suggests that the poet must struggle because God is like a giant, who cannot be explained and understood and therefore 'contained'.

Or it could mean that it is a *Divine* or God-given instinct for man to strive for more and higher knowledge. In this reading the speaker suggests that in a search for more knowledge, the poet will inevitably be wrestling with thoughts that are hard to handle or to *contain* (8), and which will inevitably threaten to overwhelm the poet as *smaller man* (12). The noun used in the second stanza, *struggle*, suggests that there will be hardship but also hopes of success.

It is interesting to think about this poem in relationship to Dickinson's views on nature. Generally she observed nature as something alien or unknowable, or even aggressive towards the human world. Here there is another perspective, and the metaphor of the parallax or varying perspectives supports this idea. The new perspective for the poet is that nature itself is not going to satisfy the need for contemplative thought; there needs to be a change of perspective. But this change can be threatening. It may be evidence of the *Divine* in man to struggle with difficult concepts, but the power to hold concepts is only as good as the mind or power of the speaker. There is a chance that it may be too bold to aim to achieve all higher thought, because while that perspective might be suitable for one of a *Giant* or God-like intellect, it may be too much for the human poet.

The last three lines offer an aphorism, emphasized by the anaphora of *And… And*. But there is still some ambiguity; might the *smaller man* be overwhelmed? Or might the *smaller man* develop into the *Giant* he lodges intellectually? Perhaps it is suggested that in taking on the role of the poet there is risk; it could either make or break the author.

There is no full stop or closure to this poem. Perhaps the speaker is directly addressing the reader, and fellow poets, giving a warning. Dickinson herself struggles in a constant battle to develop her most complex ideas.

4 **Parallax** a trick of perspectives in which the flame would disappear.

10 **Giant** it is recorded that Samuel Bowles wrote a letter to

> Dickinson from Switzerland, with an account of a similar thought. He wrote about the landscape, John Calvin (who was the founder of Calvinism upon which Puritanism was based), and God. Dickinson may have used a germ of the idea, or some of its language, to explore the parameters and problems of writing poetry.

1551 Those – dying then

In many ways this is the most devastating of Dickinson's war poems. In the first stanza she describes the state of Christian belief in her time. In the past, the speaker suggests, people knew where they were going when they died; the Bible promised they would be resurrected to sit at God's right hand. This cannot happen any more in the poet's society, for God has disappeared. Soldiers will have no reward for their sacrifice, no promise of redemption, and war is absolutely pointless as there is no divine plan for history, no hope of man using war justly.

In stanza 2 the speaker makes a comment about this. In the first two lines the loss of faith is regretted: without God there seems to be no moral or universal frame for our actions, so all that we do is seen only from a small, human perspective. There is ambiguity in these lines. They could mean that actions taken without reference to morality have no valid basis; or that immorality is so widespread it overshadows any moral concerns. Perhaps both meanings are included. The speaker concludes that it would be better to have a will o'the wisp sort of religion, a religion of appearances without any true substance, because this would at least offer mankind something to light the way. This would be better than no light at all, no guiding morality, and no hope of better things.

Again Dickinson uses contrast to present her ideas, comparing the present to a past where religion was secure, and immortality seemed certain for believers. The poem has a calm and controlled tone, which makes the content perhaps more shocking. The use of dashes maintains a sense of developing thought. There is enjambment, so both stanzas are linked as the thought develops, but the final dash, denying closure, might suggest that the speaker has no idea of what will happen in the future.

Many words are drawn from a Latinate register, and this is marked by the author's choice of the phrase *ignis fatuus* (8), rather than the more colloquial 'will o'the wisp'. This usage might suggest the solemnity of the subject matter.

This is an '*ubi sunt*' poem; the phrase means 'where are they now?', and is applied to poems in which an author bewails the loss of valuable beliefs or customs from the past. Yet Dickinson is strikingly modern in her outburst about the loss of God, anticipating the philosopher Friedrich Nietzsche's famous statement that 'God is dead'. The image she uses is shocking: the right hand of God has been amputated. Who carried out the amputation? This image does not necessarily reveal the poet's own views; might it be an attack on those who carried out the amputation? Many groups of people could be accused of this: the followers of Darwin, who denied the validity of the Genesis account of creation in the Bible; critics of religion who claimed the Bible was false; society as a whole with its increasing belief in the 'religion' of commerce and economics; and of course all this was against the background of a bloody Civil War. Then there were the Puritans who increasingly seemed to have made a God in their own image. Finally, there were the 'new' philosophers of the age, such as Thomas Carlyle, arguing for a secular reading of history. Perhaps Dickinson was a believer, in this poem presenting a ferocious attack on those who had destroyed man's relationship with God. Or perhaps she is reserving her options.

3 **God's Right Hand** according to Christian belief, when Jesus ascended to heaven after his death and resurrection he was to sit at the right hand of God to receive those among mankind whom he had redeemed. To amputate this hand is to effectively deny this doctrine.

8 **ignis fatuus** a Latinate name for a fleeting light sometimes seen hovering over marshy ground, supposedly caused by combustible gases burning; commonly known as a will o'the wisp, it was notorious for misleading night-time travellers.

1670 In Winter in my Room

This is an extraordinary, fantastical poem in which the speaker describes a terrifying encounter. In her room in winter she sees a worm; she doesn't like it so she ties it to something and leaves. On her return she sees that the worm has become a huge snake; after a cryptic dialogue she runs away, but then tells the reader that this was all a dream.

The poem is set in winter, in other words, a time of infertility. Might the idea of winter somehow relate to the poet, who is sequestered in her room away from society? There might also be a mythical level of meaning supported by Dickinson's choice of subject, a worm; in Old English or Anglo-Saxon literature, a 'worm' meant a 'dragon', a creature of threatening power.

The situation is rather absurd, but the worm is presented as disgusting, *Pink, lank and warm* (3), and the notion of tying it up is horrible. But obviously there are phallic connotations; the worm and snake seem rather like a threatening penis, maybe suggestive of a fear of men on the speaker's part. The power of the worm cannot be controlled, and it becomes a huge mottled snake: is this an erection? The eroticism of the poem links it to 213: *'Did the Harebell loose her girdle'* and 249: *'Wild Nights – Wild Nights!'*. The witty line *And worms presume* (5) would support a reading about men being pushy and seeking to dominate women. The snake therefore might be representative of masculine force, as he is *ringed with power* (17); perhaps there might be a suggestion that the emergent snake is actually a man in his true colours.

The dialogue (22–26) is presented in an ambiguous way; the speaker, presumably a woman, is afraid, so who speaks the first line? Is it the woman actually admiring the snake, or might she be flattering him out of fear? Or is it the snake who speaks, flattering her? But in a sense this does not matter, as the snake won't be put off and hisses *Afraid... Of me?* It is unclear who says *No cordiality* (26); if it is the female speaker, it might be read as a warning to the snake to keep away. Rather more threateningly, if the snake is the speaker, he implies that he has no time for courtesies, or even that it is not in his nature to take such time. That reading would be supported if the next lines are read with sexual connotations. From line 27 the register might well be sexual: *fathomed*, *Rhythm Slim*, *Secreted*, *Form*, *Patterns swim*, *Projected*. From the first *He fathomed me*, which might be an image of sexual penetration as well as implying that the snake could read her mind, these five lines could be interpreted to enact sexual intercourse and ejaculation.

A Freudian analysis would see this as the typical dream of a woman terrified by men and their threatening sexuality; or as the woman's hidden desires rising in her dreams, in which she fantasizes about sexual intercourse. Dickinson's first editors insisted that this was a purely comic poem with a humorous picture of a wide-eyed woman running away backwards from a snake; that seems a little tame nowadays, and it is difficult to believe that Dickinson did not know what she was writing. But even without the image of sexual intercourse this is a witty satire on men in society as presumptuous, vain, overbearing and threatening. Perhaps the speaker/poet has a grudging admiration for men if they are *fair* (22), but it is better to extend a *claw* (23) than a hand in *Propitiation*; in other words, always to be armed against the power of men. In this interpretation the poem is a moral fable about the attractiveness of males and the need to resist them.

There could also be a literary meaning. Winter could suggest a time of literary sterility; the worm could be an image of an evolving thought, which grows and becomes more powerful. In that reading the description of the movements in lines 28–31 could relate to literary formulations, with their rhythms and patterns. The word itself certainly has power. *That time I flew* (32) could be an image of speed in capturing these dream-like thoughts. The *distant Town* (36) would suggest a new area of thought for the writer. Or there might also be a warning about the power of the word to have a life of its own; this would relate to Mary Shelley's *Frankenstein*, where the creation proved to be too powerful for the creator. Perhaps Dickinson sounds a warning note about the power of language and the responsibilities of the writer, and therefore the *creeping blood* (13) would be a pointer to an echo of the Gothic tradition.

But there could also be a literary joke played on the reader. It is significant that the poem is set in winter: might it therefore be a winter's tale? Dickinson said that she thought the writings of Shakespeare were all anyone needed to read; might she be referring to *A Winter's Tale* here? At the beginning of the play a winter's tale is defined as being concerned with 'sprites and goblins', creatures of a mythical world in which there are also worms or dragons. She may well have used the same conventions and tropes as Shakespeare did in that play, a concern with creativity, sexuality, growth and rebirth.

All these layers of meaning are attached to this poem, but it is worth remembering that despite her high seriousness, despite the difficulties she encountered in her life, Dickinson had a sense of humour and was not above teasing her readers and setting them puzzles in trying to pin down the meaning of an extraordinary poem.

23 **Propitiation** gestures of friendship to please someone.

Interpretations

Ideas and influences in Dickinson's poetry

The Puritan religion

Emily Dickinson was born into a fairly wealthy family whose members adhered to the strict codes of Puritanism which was developed from Calvinism in the mid-sixteenth century. During the reign of James I of England, the nation became increasingly hostile to the practices of Puritanism, believing that is caused serial unrest. Feeling threatened, a group of Congregationalists left England in the 1620s to settle at Plymouth in America. A later and more powerful party settled the Massachusetts Bay area in 1630; this group had a charter for self-rule granted by Charles I, and appointed the intelligent and powerful John Winthrop as governor. It is from these mixed roots that New England Puritanism was formed.

The Puritans sought to free the Anglican Church from excessive rituals such as the cult of the Virgin Mary, the use of Latin, candles, incense and elaborate ceremonies with elaborate garments, and also to free themselves from the powerful hierarchy of bishops. They wished to reclaim the scholarly texts used to support religious argument, and the number of sacraments was reduced from the seven of the Catholic Church to just two, baptism and marriage. They believed in plainness and simplicity even in their sermons; Dickinson mocks Anglican excess in 315: *'He fumbles at your Soul'*.

From Calvinism the Puritans adopted the idea of Predestination, that God would choose those to be saved (the 'Elect') even before their lives began. This decision was irreversible, and no amount of good behaviour or good works could change an adverse decision. God was perceived as unknown and unknowable. The 'Elect' would at some point experience the 'conversion', a sense of inner assurance of God's grace. This was known as 'justification', and their subsequent behaviour was therefore 'sanctified'.

It was a harsh religion to live by; the behavioural code was severe. But the benefit was that this 'conversion' could occur at any point in a life, so it was not a wholly pessimistic religion. A second optimistic factor was that Puritans believed God had a divine plan for human history leading to universal salvation, in which everyone had a part to play. History would assuredly turn out well for mankind.

Underpinning the Puritan faith were three Covenants: that of Work, which Adam broke when he disobeyed God, but which was re-made with Abraham; the Covenant of Redemption, in which Jesus died on the cross to redeem man from original sin and allow for salvation; and the Covenant of Grace, in which there was seen to be a contract with God according to which due punishment for sin was accepted.

Churches were self-governing and autonomous, with power divided between the pastor, the teacher, the elders, and the deacon. The Puritans believed that the state should actively intervene to enforce strict codes of moral behaviour by banning such things as drinking, swearing, gambling and fashionable, showy dress, and insisting on strict observation of the Sabbath.

During the nineteenth century, Puritanism was still very strong in Amherst. Waves of religious fervour continued to sweep through New England, and the Second Great Revival caught up Dickinson in its wake. She had been sent to Mount Holyoke Female Seminary in 1847, where the headmistress was a fervent believer who pressed her students into experiencing 'conversion'. Three groups of students were established in the college: those who were very likely to convert; those who may convert; and the 'no-hopers', into which group Dickinson was placed. Always honest with herself, she felt that she had too many reservations to commit herself, and she mistrusted social pressures (and even more so mass hysteria). It was perhaps because of this pressure that she left after one year, half way through her course.

Her home would have been typical of a good Puritan family

home. Prayers were spoken together, hymns were sung daily, and Sundays would be set aside for church and for devotional thought. At first Dickinson did go to church with her family; but she increasingly withdrew from this practice. Nevertheless, she was known to have enjoyed the sermons of the modern type of preacher with the 'hell-raiser' and 'firebrand' style. Such preachers as the Reverend Charles Wadsworth were skilled, intellectual and persuasive, swaying the congregation to their point of view by drawing examples from everyday life rather than from the scriptures. This method could be seen to some degree as a secularization of religious thought, and may have influenced Dickinson to think similarly.

Despite the pleasure of the sermons, she began to absent herself from the Sunday service, and on one occasion her father called in the doctor to check if she were really ill. Finally she abandoned church-going altogether; she wrote a poem about refusing to go to church. Nevertheless, she observed the behavioural code for the Sabbath and instead of writing poetry she wrote her private letters.

The influence of this religion on her poetry is enormous and evident everywhere, and she called the topics of religion, death, and immortality her 'Flood Subjects'. Like the Reverend Charles Wadsworth, she secularized religious language, but for a different purpose. She was openly critical of some aspects of current religious practice.

From the family's hymn singing she developed an affection for common metre, the metre of hymns, which she often uses in her poetry. She makes frequent allusions to the Bible, especially the Book of Revelation, which speaks so vividly of the glories of the world to come. However, she had real doubts about the ways in which Puritans were behaving; she felt that they had created a God very much in their own likeness, and that church members were at times hypocritical and back-biting. She was also troubled that they equated material and financial success with moral goodness and believed that worldly success indicated that a person was of the 'Elect'.

Activity

Religious concerns are often present in the poetry of Emily Dickinson. Discuss some examples.

Discussion

Many poems could be selected for this discussion – here are three examples for you to develop.

In 216: *'Safe in their Alabaster Chambers'*, she is critical of the show of wealth displayed in the tombs, and certainly did not see this as a promise of redemption and salvation. She probably mocks the rituals attached to death in 465: *'I heard a Fly buzz – when I died'*, and there is probably a satire on contemporary religious excesses in 1068: *'Further in Summer than the Birds'*. Throughout her poetry we find the register of the Puritan religion: 'Elect', 'Divine Majority', 'Ordinance', 'Communion', 'Mass' and 'Canticle', for example.

There is a need for caution in assessing Dickinson's attitude to religion and to the existence of God. It is generally not clear whether she is sceptical about the doctrines, or critical of Puritan excesses and arrogance. It is impossible to know exactly what she believed and thought; in her last, brief letter, written to her cousins the day before she died, she states simply and movingly that she has been 'called back'. This does rather suggest that she viewed life on earth as an interruption in another life, presumably in heaven. Or perhaps she was simply not sure about this.

The Civil War and social change

New England, with the universities of Yale and Harvard, has always been the intellectual capital of America, so towns such as Boston, Concord and Amherst had some significance. In Dickinson's lifetime social change was happening as rapidly in America as in England, so for the much younger nation the time span from its foundation to becoming a leading economic power was much more compressed. This must have made life energetic but also disorienting and confusing, as the northern and southern states began to make different responses to change.

Traditionally, New Englanders were Republicans, representing, as Dickinson's family did, the 'old' aristocracy of the United States. But at the turn of the nineteenth century social problems arose. In 1831 the first slave rebellion happened; there was an economic depression in 1837; and in 1850 the Compromise Bill addressed the problem of slavery but only in the territories. The rise of the Democratic Party was evident. Dickinson picks up some of these pressures in 288: *'I'm Nobody! Who are you?'*. Two movements were developing simultaneously: the drive towards the freedom of the individual, exemplified in the growing women's rights movement, with its first convention in 1848; and increasing economic and commercial pressures, which threatened to crush the individual and lead to exploitation by capitalist entrepreneurs, such as John Singer, who established the first Singer sewing machine company in 1861. Society was becoming democratized, helped by the immigration in 1845 of many Irish people after the potato famine in Ireland. In 1853 the great railway opened a line to Amherst, which was symbolic of the new times.

Against this background the Civil War broke out, initially as a war of ideologies; both sides, the northern states of the Federal Union and the southern states to be known later as Confederates, claimed to be acting for justice. The southern states felt that they were despised by the North as plantation owners and for their reliance on slavery, but they did not believe that the northern states would put the Federal Union at risk by going to war with the South. Similarly, the northern states did not believe that the southern states would go to war over the matter of slavery, and thought their threat of secession from the union was a bluff. Both called each other's bluff; in February 1861 under the leadership of Jefferson Davis a confederation of southern states was declared. In April the town of Charleston was attacked by the confederalists, and Virginia, Arkansas, Tennessee and North Carolina also seceded. War between the unionists of the North and confederalists of the South began in earnest.

The war became increasingly savage as families were divided so that father and son, brother and brother might be fighting each other. The war lasted until 1865; it is reflected in Dickinson's poetry directly in poems such as 690: '*Victory comes late*' and 67: '*Success is counted sweetest*', and indirectly in many others, since the register of war is applied to other areas. The idea of the battlefield pervades much of her poetry. She engages in dispute between opposing claims; her poetry is dramatic in form, and conflict lies at the root of drama. The Civil War becomes the symbol for all that was wrong in nineteenth-century America: increasing commercialism, financial pressures, the formation of large corporations with underpaid workforces, and above all a Puritan church which to Dickinson seemed to be far more concerned with its relationship to society than to God. Thus the Civil War could be seen to represent the warring elements which she believed were tearing society apart.

Activity

Many critics see Dickinson as an anti-war poet. How do you respond to this idea?

Discussion

You could select three poems and assess what they reveal about her views, for example 67: 'Success is counted sweetest', 444: '*It feels a shame to be Alive*', and 690: '*Victory comes late*'. In the first, you might explore the paradox offered – that there can be no winner in war. With 444, you might find the tone harsher, indicated by the dominant image of bodies piled up *like Dollars*. In 690, you might consider that there is an even harsher image of God denying sustenance. The poet's comment that *Victory comes late* raises the question of whether there is any point in victory, and therefore in war, when all mankind is suffering for lack of love or care. What do you think the poet believes?

Women in nineteenth-century America

Dickinson's father's attitudes to women were typical in New England. Believing in the right of women to be educated, he sent his daughter to Amherst Academy in 1840–1847, and then to Mount Holyoke Female Seminary. However, he made it known that he did not think women should be over-educated in case this jeopardized their marriage prospects. He declared these views publicly in articles for the local paper in 1826–1827.

Although the women's rights movement had held its first convention in 1848, no real effects had reached Amherst. Women were expected to marry, and to take an important but subordinate role supporting their husbands. Dickinson's attitude to this is clear in poems such as 732: *'She rose to His Requirement – dropt'* and 199: *'I'm "wife" – I've finished that'*. Although she had love affairs, she remained unmarried.

A second difficulty for Dickinson as a woman was the problem of making her way as a professional writer. Some contemporary American women had managed to do this, such as Louisa M. Alcott, the author of *Little Women*, and Harriet Beecher Stowe who wrote *Uncle Tom's Cabin*. Perhaps if it had been financially necessary to write the problem would have disappeared. But Dickinson did not need to support herself by writing. After reading an article in the *Atlantic Monthly* of spring 1862, which gave advice to would-be poets, she sent four of her poems to the author, Thomas Wentworth Higginson. It was this chance event that changed the course of Dickinson's life, as a close, life-long literary relationship began between the former Unitarian minister and the young poet. He supported her writing, but advised her not to go into print. He was to become the first co-editor of her poems after her death.

Dickinson had a dozen poems published in local papers in her lifetime, sent over 500 to friends, and sewed the rest of her poems into bundles called 'fascicles' or gatherings. She felt forced into a compromise which finally led to her social withdrawal and the wearing of white. She probably considers this situation in poems such as 657: '*I dwell in Possibility*'. Through her poems she explores issues related to women in society and works in quiet rebellion by claiming the right to enter traditionally male areas of practice and thought.

Activity

At several points in her poetry Dickinson suggests the difficulties of her position as a female poet. How does she express such problems?

Discussion

You could take as a starting point 732: 'She rose to His Requirement – dropt', where the problems of being a woman generally are articulated through natural imagery. Then move on to 709: 'Publication – is the Auction', which uses the language of commerce and publishing to set out her concerns. A third helpful poem might be 327: 'Before I got my eye put out', where she articulates her final choices using social, material and literary imagery.

Thomas Wentworth Higginson, who supported Dickinson's work

Dickinson's sense of history

A traditional Christian and Puritan view of history is that a redemptive scheme is unfolding behind historic development. According to such a view, God will take care of mankind in the course of human history; progress will gradually lead man towards redemption and salvation in heaven. Jesus's death and resurrection redeemed man from deadly sin. Of course man had to live in an appropriate, moral way. In such a scheme, war would be seen as necessary as long as it was just; it was a necessary evil to purify the human race and ensure that the course of history led to redemption.

It would seem that Dickinson did not share this idea of history at all, and would have nothing to do with such a theory. The Civil War brought suffering to the nation and to some friends such as Frazar Stearns, whom she knew from college. She saw nothing glorious or redemptive in it, as can be seen in poems such as 1183: '*Step lightly on this narrow spot*', and 444: '*It feels a shame to be Alive*'. She adopted an alternative view of history, seeming to take God out of the equation. This may be partly due to the influence of preachers such as Reverend Charles Wadsworth, who had similarly secularized religious ideas in his sermons to make them shock his audience and strike home. However, it could also be due to the influence of the ideas of Thomas Carlyle, a Scottish philosopher. Dickinson had a picture of Carlyle on her bedroom wall, and the family owned a copy of *On Heroes, Hero-Worship and the Heroic in History*, published in 1841, from which her brother quoted in an inaugural speech at Amherst College. There was a copy of Carlyle's *The French Revolution*, written in 1837, in Amherst library which Dickinson's sister Lavinia borrowed. Tantalizingly, there are pencil markings on some of the pages, but the handwriting cannot be identified as that of the poet.

Another clear route for her knowledge of the writings and ideas of Carlyle is through her reading of Ralph Waldo Emerson's writings. Emerson was indebted to Carlyle for some

Thomas Carlyle, the Scottish philosopher
whose work influenced Dickinson

of his ideas, and he visited the Scottish philosopher in Europe in 1833. Benjamin Franklin Newton gave Dickinson a copy of Emerson's poems in 1850. Dickinson and Newton were very close. Dickinson always called the clerk her 'tutor', and it is recorded that he inspired her with new ideas. A third route may have been through the writings of John Ruskin, which Dickinson had read; Ruskin was a friend and a disciple of Carlyle.

In *On Heroes, Hero-Worship and the Heroic in History*, Carlyle explored the idea of the great man as the agent of historical change, and the importance of myths related to such men in establishing national development; he firmly linked the myths to these men rather than to God. Carlyle believed in the fusion of events, in the coming together of the right man and the right moment for change; this idea of 'fusion' is a characteristic of Dickinson's poetic processes. In *The French Revolution*, Carlyle portrayed a situation in France which was similar to that in America at the time: the older aristocracy had begun to falter while a newer and more vigorous democracy threatened. Carlyle saw history as a series of cycles, impelled by great men, but with societies inevitably collapsing until a phoenix rises out of the ashes and the whole cycle begins again. Man, not God, is the agent of historical change.

Carlyle also expressed his disapproval of the principles his contemporary society appeared to have adopted; he believed that society worked on a 'cash nexus', that money, power, trade and commerce were the basis of society. It is clear that Dickinson shared this view, for example in her reference to the lives *like Dollars... piled*, in 444: *'It feels a shame to be Alive'*. In poems such as 1551: *'Those – dying then'*, God is not just absent or omitted from the poem, his right hand is *amputated*. If God's right hand is no longer there, then neither can Jesus be.

Dickinson as a Romantic poet

To some extent Dickinson is a Romantic poet. The Romantics were a group of poets spearheaded by William Wordsworth and Samuel Taylor Coleridge who rebelled against the literature of the eighteenth century. They objected to the perception of reason as more significant than emotion; they disliked the obsession with balance, order and symmetry in writing, feeling that it was unnatural and not the true voice of humanity. Their attack began with the publication of *Lyrical Ballads*, with its important Preface, in 1798. They believed that emotion was more important than reason; that the language used should be the natural language of the people; that strong emotion was appropriate for poetry; that the poet must write in a situation outside of society; and that scientific analysis was less valuable than intuition fuelled by the senses. The extreme sensuousness of Romantic poetry is evident in John Keats's writing, such as *Ode to a Nightingale*, where poetry is seen to emerge as a product of sensuous hallucination.

There is much evidence of sensuousness in Dickinson's poetry from the early 211: *'Come slowly – Eden!'* to the later 1068: *'Further in Summer than the Birds'*, where a near-hallucinatory trance is induced by responding to the senses. Romantic poetry was inevitably often subjective, an exploration of the poets' ideas and feelings, and they thought that nature should be man's great guide and teacher.

Dickinson wrote from a standpoint of isolation, and she rejected and criticized the growing power of money and status in society, as is evident in poems such as 709: '*Publication – is the Auction*'. Believing in the centrally Romantic notion of the necessity for self-knowledge, she often explored her feelings, especially in the 'Poems of Definition' such as 341: '*After great pain, a formal feeling comes*', and she frequently expressed joy and ecstasy in poems such as 249: '*Wild Nights – Wild Nights!*'. However, the true Romantic poet believed in the power of nature, and although Dickinson paid some lip-service to this idea in poems such as 668: '"*Nature" is what we see*', she broke away from this area of thought.

Activity

Compare and contrast 414: *''Twas like a Maelstrom, with a notch' with 657: 'I dwell in Possibility'* as Romantic poems.

Discussion

There are three ways of handling comparisons: analysing each poem separately and carrying out the comparison at the end; moving across the poems continually; or dividing the work into sections such as 'Themes', 'Images', etc. and moving across at the end of each section. To adopt the third method, consider first the top level of meaning in each poem: who is the subject of the poem? Is it the 'I' persona so popular in Romantic poetry? Consider the themes, exploring how the individual achieves identity by surviving trauma and defining it, or by thinking deeply about the choice of writing poetry, both of which are centrally Romantic themes. Consider finally the methods used in the striking and dramatic imagery, in accordance with the imaginative excess of much Romantic poetry. Conclude by offering an opinion on the degree to which each is a 'Romantic poem'.

Transcendentalism in Dickinson's poetry

To some extent Dickinson followed the ideas of Transcendentalism. Ralph Waldo Emerson, who lived in nearby Concord, and his follower Henry David Thoreau were the leaders of American Transcendental thought; they taught that man should be self-sufficient and not conform to the rules and regulations of society. In this area Dickinson is a true follower. However, Emerson developed the idea more fully, teaching that men could unite in harmony through nature in the 'Great Oversoul', transcending differences. Once again Dickinson had to stop short of full agreement.

Existentialism in Dickinson's poetry

Existentialism became popular through the writings of Jean-Paul Sartre in the early to mid twentieth century, but Dickinson anticipated this movement. Existentialism advocates a *carpe diem*, live-for-the-moment attitude to life, and certainly she appeared to project a philosophy in which life on earth and its mental, physical and spiritual pleasures are all-important. It is the here and now that seems to matter, and not a life after death, whenever and wherever that may be. Following on from this philosophy is the idea that people must be as much in control of their destiny as possible, and to achieve this they must understand their own situation.

In many of her poems such as 79: '*Going to Heaven!*', 214: '*I taste a liquor never brewed*', 216: '*Safe in their Alabaster Chambers*', and 258: '*There's a certain Slant of light*', Dickinson shows a preference for the sensuous life on earth over some vague, distant and unprovable theory of redemption and salvation. This is perhaps another reason why religious language and tropes are wrenched from their religious context and related to the human condition and to nature.

The Gothic genre

Gothic features are used in some of Dickinson's poems, especially in Fascicle 16 and some of 17, from which this selection is drawn. She would have become familiar with this tradition through novels such as Mary Shelley's *Frankenstein* (1818), and Edgar Allan Poe's works such as *The Fall of the House of Usher* (1839) and *The Raven* (1845). Dickinson adopted many of the characteristics of this genre to create various effects in her poems. These include the use of a dark or night setting; creation of suspense, often by repetition and rhythm; eerie or shocking sound effects; a confusion of the senses; a disturbed and disturbing situation; and a passive or helpless female victim.

The use of this genre creates many effects; it acts as a signpost to the reader, who knows what to expect and becomes sympathetically attuned. Gothic effects give a poem dramatic vividness, heighten the horror of a physical situation and also the different thematic levels of meaning, and force the reader to attend. They also rest upon a secular mode of thought.

Activity

Compare the presentation of dying in two poems, 280: *'I felt a Funeral, in my Brain'* and 1100: *'The last Night that She lived'*.

Discussion

This exercise will clearly show the effects of the use of the Gothic genre. It might be better to work through the two poems separately here, since they are so dissimilar. Work through the first by checking the Gothic characteristics outlined above against the poem to see how fully and how fluently Dickinson uses this genre. On the first level of meaning, that of a funeral, the use of the Gothic builds a suspense which becomes anticlimactic when the plank breaks. The second level of meaning, a descent into madness, works differently, as the plank of reason breaking is even more dramatic than the literal meaning.

It is worth considering whether the use of the Gothic genre is an indication that God has been omitted, as the thoughts are entirely secularized. In comparison, the second poem seems to be very

controlled, equally suspenseful perhaps, but deliberately more flat. Or is it? When death comes, there is really nothing left. This is an equally secular poem since death is quite obviously the end of everything.

The influence of metaphysical poetry

Dickinson's poetry exhibits many of the features of metaphysical poetry. This label is given to the poetry of Christian writers of the seventeenth century such as John Donne, George Herbert and Andrew Marvell, and it was just as shocking to readers of the age as Dickinson's poetry was to her contemporary or near-contemporary readers. Techniques that Dickinson has in common with the metaphysical poets include the use of the intensely personal lyric form; shocking and startling openings; the evidence of unusual thoughts in 'normal' situations; very compressed language, often with terms drawn from geography and science; and above all, the use of **conceits**. These are particularly effective images which force readers to see a likeness in things not apparently alike.

The compression of her thought, the initial shock to grab the reader's attention and the aptness of unusual images is seen in poems such as 254: '*"Hope" is the thing with feathers*'. The use of this genre adds humour and sparkle to her poems, and helps to make a profound point clear, as in 512: '*The Soul has Bandaged moments*'. Some readers think that because Dickinson does not have a clear Christian faith, she cannot be regarded as an heir to the metaphysical poets; but she may have the faith, and she certainly has the deep understanding of it.

Activity

Analyse line 10 of 1072: *'Title divine – is mine!'*

Discussion

It is very difficult to summarize, let alone paraphrase, Dickinson's poetry because of its compression. Here the argument against marriage is revealed in just three words. It would be interesting to

move on to 732: *'She rose to His Requirement – dropt'* and attempt a paraphrase of stanzas 2 and 3. Such exercises as these will help you analyse her poetic skills.

The dramatic monologue

Dickinson was a great admirer of the master of the dramatic monologue, Robert Browning, who published *Men and Women* in 1855 and *Dramatis Personae* in 1864. He created an array of vivid characters, mostly sinful or arrogant people, entirely without self-knowledge. As the characters speak directly, appealing to the reader for sympathy, they reveal themselves in their true colours.

The dramatic monologue form allows for complexity in many ways; there is a speaker or persona who could in various roles represent the poet; the speaker acts as a mediator between reader and poet; the voice may be shrouded in secrecy so that the views expressed do not offend; a female poet can assume a man's role and voice; and the persona can explore a situation interesting to the poet.

Robert Browning, of whose dramatic monologues Dickinson was a great admirer

The differing perspectives offer a wonderful vehicle for irony. A gentle irony is evident in 79: '*Going to Heaven!*', where a child-like speaker is seen and heard growing up before the reader's eyes. The anonymous persona of 199: '*I'm "wife" – I've finished that*' can implicitly condemn men, marriage and social customs. Throughout, the dramatic monologues entertain on many levels, and they allow Dickinson to say many things that society would not have tolerated if said in her own voice.

Activity

Compare two dramatic monologues, 288: *'I'm Nobody! Who are you?'* and 712: *'Because I could not stop for Death'*, to assess the effectiveness of Dickinson's use of the dramatic monologue form.

Discussion

Compare first the purposes of the two poems. The first is very much concerned with the state of a society which is economically and commercially based. The second poem, in contrast, deals with death; because it seems to be much gentler in tone, the reader is touched. The persona can see life and the loss of life, but bleakly can see nothing after death. The roles of the speakers compare well; in the first, the persona directly harangues the reader, cajoling and persuading. In the second, the reader is seduced by the gentle voice, perhaps of a Southern belle being chivalrously courted. The kick comes at the end. It would be worth thinking about the relationship of the poet to the poem – at what remove is she from the poem?

Lyrical poetry

Dickinson often wrote lyrics; these are song-like poems, usually fairly short. It is a subjective form, often with an 'I' persona exploring identity and selfhood, and the emotions of the author – or of the persona. As such it was a form much used by the metaphysical poets and the Romantics, such as Wordsworth, who defined a lyric as the outpouring of strong emotions. A fine example of the lyric is 211: '*Come slowly – Eden!*'

Themes in Dickinson's poetry

Themes reflect the central concerns of the author. There is a need for caution here, as what an individual reader might perceive as central, or ideas that a reader from a different time period or society from the author selects, may not be the same concerns as the author intended to explore. Concerns may have arisen entirely without authorial purpose: words have a life of their own. It is worth remembering that just as different readers take different meanings from a poem, so will they deduce different themes. It is necessary to be aware of the multiplicity of meanings that can arise from a text.

The unity of Dickinson's poetry

Before fragmenting the selected poems by following discrete themes, it is worth considering the unity of thought in Dickinson's poetry. Uniting all her poems in one central concern is the quest for identity and for selfhood.

The motif of the quest has always been important in literature, from the quest of the ancient Greek Odysseus, through the medieval period and the Arthurian legends, to modern times with J.R.R. Tolkien's *Lord of the Rings*, and J.K. Rowling's *Harry Potter* tales. This is a natural area of enquiry for a Romantic poet, and it is the driving force for Dickinson's search for identity and selfhood throughout her poetry.

This quest has profound effects on not just the subject matter, but the method also. During a search, it is inevitable that a person views and rejects alternatives, or opposing situations or ways of thinking. That process is essential in order to make a choice. Looking through Dickinson's poetry it becomes obvious that nearly all of her poems are based on oppositions or alternatives, which are seldom reconciled. Generally she leaves the reader to make the choices, as her 'self' emerges in a composite picture. However, some decisions are taken, as in 327: '*Before I got my eye put out*'. But then the veil comes over the poem: there is a tentative mood, and the effectiveness of the choice is not further demonstrated.

You will see a similar process in other areas; 216: *'Safe in their Alabaster Chambers'* uses this binary system in a contemplation about death; 640: *'I cannot live with You'* applies the system to human love; 668: *'"Nature" is what we see'* offers a formal debate. It is by looking at all perspectives that knowledge may be gained.

Dickinson's poetry was in many ways a quest for certainties about life, and an attempt to define experiences specifically to gain self-knowledge. In 510: *'It was not Death, for I stood up'*, the poet works through a series of negatives, rather like checking off a list. The 'Poems of Definition' as a group are good examples of quest poems.

There are certain 'crossroads' poems which combine most of the different themes together; such poems include 690:*'Victory comes late'*, 1072: *'Title divine – is mine!'*, and 1551: *'Those – dying then'*. It is worth analysing them to assess the importance of the quest in the unifying themes.

There are many poems about war as a general principle, which together with the basis of conflict in her poetry might suggest that the quest is not just personal. Dickinson universalizes a search for a new role for women in society, and in doing so quietly rebels against and subverts traditional power and authority. In the discussion of rhyme on page 181, we see that she uses the very form of the poem as well as the content to further this.

Activity

Consider as an example of a 'crossroads' poem about a quest, 1551: *'Those – dying then'*.

Discussion

The poem invites consideration of all the major themes. In the relationship of the individual to the state it is obvious the state does

not value individuals, as otherwise there would be no inglorious death, as suggested here by the comparison with the past; nature is unhelpful as her *ignis fatuus* misleads people. God has deserted mankind – or has he? Could it be that society has formed the wrong impression of God, that the Puritans have foolishly cast him in their own likeness? As ever, there is a quest for certainties in social and religious life; these questions remain unanswered, but issues of practice and belief have been raised.

Death and immortality

Dickinson called issues related to death and immortality her 'Flood Subjects', which might suggest that her mind was overwhelmed by the complexities of these concepts. The conclusions she presents seem to suggest that death is unknown and unknowable. Despite the repeated treatment of the topic in her poetry, all explorations of dying and of death remain fixed within the confines of the human mind.

She presents the topic of death from many different perspectives. In 280: *'I felt a Funeral, in my Brain'*, the speaker on the literal level seems to be the dead woman recounting her death up to the point where a plank breaks over the grave shaft and the coffin falls into the hole, in a style reflecting the Gothic tradition. Read as an account of developing madness, the poem is not about death but about dying, as are 465: *'I heard a Fly buzz – when I died'*, and 1100: *'The last Night that She lived'*.

The first of these poems is at least as grotesque as *'I felt a Funeral, in my Brain'*. The victim is horribly coherent as she watches the rites of passage into death. The weeping and the will-signing are all clearly and detachedly observed. When the fly appears, the poem becomes horrific: it is a blue fly, the type that may lay its eggs on the corpse to develop into maggots. Ironically, or perhaps fortuitously, the woman cannot see anything further. That is left to the reader's imagination.

The tone of *'The last Night that She lived'* is totally different, but equally effective. An observer records the dying process in a detached way. She or he is struck by the passivity of the dying woman; in the face of this, the watchers try to keep busy.

This is shown in a different way in 712: '*Because I could not stop for Death*'. The speaker seems pleased when the courteous gentleman conducts her on a journey through the different stages of life, through time, to the grave. They head for *Eternity*, but of course it is not reached. The shadowy third character in the coach, *Immortality*, is not mentioned again. Once more, it would seem that there is nothing after death; all the life that matters is on earth.

Several poems contain ideas about immortality. In 216: '*Safe in their Alabaster Chambers*', the speaker contemplates a tomb. What is absolutely clear in both versions is that the tomb will contain the people eternally. It is their home; they are sequestered from the processes of life in the first version, and even more strongly from the concepts of time and space in the second version. There is no sense at any point in the poems that they will join the saints in heaven; in fact they are satirized for assuming this. In 79: '*Going to Heaven!*' the speaker, assuming a child's voice, talks of going to heaven as a comfortable process that will happen one day. There will be a new little robe and crown, but it will be just like going home after a trip out. Suddenly the mask drops at the first line of the third stanza: there seems to be a clear preference now for staying on earth, and the angered tone emphasizes this point. As with death, immortality is unknown and unknowable.

However, in 322:'*There came a Day at Summer's full*', there is a glimpse of a sort of paradise; and there is a type of immortality in 214: '*I taste a liquor never brewed*', where angels and saints are drawn into the everlasting joys of life. What emerges is the view that immortality is a continuation of the joys of life. Dickinson once asked a friend whether claims for immortality were true; it was a question that stayed with her throughout her life, but she could find no suitable evidence for it or any analogy to define it in any other way than in earthly terms.

Activity

Consider the question 'What ideas does Dickinson present about death and immortality?'.

Discussion

The idea of death is presented from several perspectives, but humans can only get so far in their knowledge. Death is unknown and unknowable.

However, where there is a faith it is different. Believers are comforted by doctrines such as salvation, redemption and resurrection. The watchers in 465: *'I heard a Fly buzz – when I died'* are poised and still, as the poem explains, waiting for the *King* to come. They expect a significant event or perhaps a signal from God; something to indicate that there really is more beyond this life. To support this reading, the language devices include Gothic elements, manipulation of line and metre, and the use of dashes to create suspense. But it is made clear that nothing happens; the poem ends with the death. There is no evidence of a different type of life after death.

In 322: *'There came a Day at Summer's full'*, the presentation of a ritualized and sacred love offers promise; in 214: *'I taste a liquor never brewed'* the sheer exuberance and vitality of life on earth clearly outweighs the promise of a life in heaven as traditionally described. Immortality is of a human kind: an extension of the best of life on earth.

Consider how the idea of immortality is presented in 501: *'This World is not Conclusion'*. In this poem a different type of presentation is used. It would be worthwhile to compare the methods used in this poem with those used in *'I taste a liquor never brewed'*, and decide what, if any, are the differences in the views offered.

Religion and God

The views on death and immortality presented in the poems lead on to the views on religion and God. In the war poems, God's absence is underlined. In 690: '*Victory comes late*' and 1551: '*Those – dying then*', God's failure to keep his promise to mankind is absolutely plain. In the first of these, the image of the bird table draws on Psalm 23, the Sermon on the Mount, and also the Prayer of Humble Access from the communion service. Perhaps the reference to the communion prayer, which churchgoers say before going up to receive communion from the altar, is the most damning of all; here men come also to God's table but they are either starved or choked. Perhaps they choke at a sense of their own folly?

In 1551: '*Those – dying then*', the speaker is even less guarded. In this bleak picture there is simply no religion left at all, no theology in which to trust. In 444: '*It feels a shame to be Alive*', all the parameters defined by faith dissolve. There is clearly no defined godhead, which leaves a space for a new sort of divinity; this may be why in the poem the brave soldiers become the new *Saviors*, the new *Divinity*.

Taking a different approach in 501: '*This World is not Conclusion*', the attack is aimed to appeal to the reader's intellect rather than the heart and the emotions, as in the war poems. The poem concludes with the thought that there will always be a doubt niggling away. However, all these views are the views of the speakers of the poems, and are not presented as Dickinson's own views.

Activity

Consider the idea that Dickinson quarrels with her God throughout her poetry.

Discussion

It is possible that Dickinson sought to confront her fears about her faith and about God in her poetry. The poems are often presented as a series of battles between faith and doubt, and clearly the topic of war is ideal for raising this issue. Finally her views must remain unknown, but it is worth remembering that humans often quarrel with those closest to them.

As well as in the war poems and the poems about religion and death, religious language is secularized throughout Dickinson's poetry, in an often cryptic way. Religious images are constantly

hijacked to serve human purposes. Love and nature are presented in religious terms, and almost as religious rituals. Might this suggest that Dickinson is relocating religious truths in the heart of man, in human nature? Or might she be suggesting sometimes that the human race has the wrong image of God? People have made a God in their own likeness, caught up in their own ignorance and folly. Perhaps God is as John Calvin defined him, unknown and unknowable?

Love

It is worth treating the topic of love separately from the topic of marriage because there is such a clear divide in Dickinson's mind. Love is a wide topic and includes love of another person; love of God; love of country; and love of life. Here the discussion will be centred on human love.

Dickinson presents several types of human love in her poetry. In 211: *'Come slowly – Eden!'* the tone is playfully erotic. Love and sex are presented as joyous and natural. To make her point clearly, she uses an extended natural image of a bee entering a flower, probably to represent the sexual act. The choice of language exempts the author from charges of improper subject matter. After all, this is a poem about a bee and a flower, and if a reader says otherwise, who bears the blame? The language of nature is gentle, indirect, and non-sexual so will cause no offence to readers. The same could be claimed for 249: '*Wild Nights – Wild Nights!*'. This is a more overtly sexual poem – perhaps. Or is it simply an account of a sailor's dream, or of a dangerous voyage on a stormy sea? Certainly her editor Thomas Higginson thought it was innocent.

Love is also seen as the natural end of a journey. In 322: '*There came a Day at Summer's full*', love is presented in a sacramental, ritualized way supported by the use of religious images and language. Love replaces the act of communion in church; it is a communion between lovers. For lovers, it is indeed a sacrament, enriching and fulfilling. Yes, there will be pain attached to it, *Calvaries* to bear, but there is no doubt that this love will be rewarded by immortality. Is earthly love a type of the divine love of God, or in fact has the divine love of God been replaced and re-rooted within and not outside of the human head and heart?

Love is not always presented in such an elevated way. In 446: '*I showed her Heights she never saw*', Dickinson seems to present love as a battle of the sexes. As the first line suggests, this is a poem about seeing and not seeing, about perspective and illusion. There are many possibilities in this poem; it could be about gay love, but with all the Gothic tricks and interplay of perspectives such a reading could never be proved. Perhaps Dickinson plays the male role as a warning to women about men. The use of italics and dialogue objectifies and distances the poem as a little drama emerges.

Finally there is the teasing fun of 1670: '*In Winter in my Room*'. We have no love poem that is unambiguously about a specific love for a specific person, so as far as the author is concerned, the poems remain impersonal and universal.

Nature

Dickinson did not subscribe to the Romantic view of nature being in sympathy with human beings. Although she paid deference to nature and appreciated natural beauty, the dominant impression gained from her poetry is that nature is of a different order from man. In fact nature might be seen as alien, or even aggressive.

Nor did she subscribe to the Transcendental view that regarded nature as a wise teacher and moral guide. She is not a poet of nature like Wordsworth; her central interest is mankind in various contexts: social, moral, emotional, theological and natural.

It would seem that Dickinson proposes a definition of nature in 668: '*"Nature" is what we see*'. However, the purpose could be the very opposite of this, as she seems to conclude that *Nature* is finally elusive and cannot be defined. The poet defines three areas of consideration through the use of dialogue: what we see; what we hear; and what we know intuitively, but cannot express. The conclusion seems to be that while we know certain aspects of nature through our senses, it is essentially unknowable because of its simplicity. It is possible that Dickinson is implying that God gave nature this simplicity and therefore only God can truly know nature.

The world of nature is admired in 328: '*A Bird came down the Walk*'. The velvety head, the bright eyes and the easy flight are described sympathetically, but there is a gulf between man and nature in this poem; the bird's eating habits seem none too pleasant to a human. More than that, the bird will not tolerate human intervention. Not only are the two worlds distinct, but as in the previous poem, it is clear that humans can never penetrate the mysteries nature holds.

Frequently nature can be hostile or threatening to man, as in 986: '*A narrow Fellow in the Grass*'. The speaker is happy to discuss the appearance and habits of the snake but the truth is that this creature instils fear, makes him *Zero at the Bone*.

Dickinson appears to begin to explain her attitude to nature in 1286: '*I thought that nature was enough*', but again this is not sustained. Here the landscape represents the gateway to other thoughts; she begins to think possibly of God as maker of the universe, then goes on to wonder how much capacity for abstract thought we humans have. Nature is the trigger for conceptual thought.

Dickinson makes great use of nature in her poetry and at times she presents nature in a sacramental way, as in 258: '*There's a certain Slant of light*'. This description of oblique and beautiful light works in an existential way to stress the value of man's life on earth in the face of mutability, at the expense of salvation and heaven. Another poem in which she works similarly is 1068: '*Further in Summer than the Birds*'.

Poems that appear to start out by describing nature are in fact used to reveal something about man and his condition. Nature is also used to express an internal landscape, as in 249: '*Wild Nights – Wild Nights!*', where the dangerous seas of the dreadful storm suggest what is happening in the mind of the speaker. Or she may use natural landscape as a trigger for human emotions. In 732: *'She rose to His Requirement – dropt'*, elements of nature in the form of precious metals and underwater treasures are used in a Shakespearean way to represent many things that go on in the depths of a married woman's mind.

In the strange poem 1670: *'In Winter in my Room'*, the reference to the seasons and also to the worm and snake are focuses of interest for the reader, as these references are central in opening up a variety of readings for the poem. Elsewhere Dickinson uses nature to establish an opposition between the tangible pleasures of earthly life and the unknown processes that happen after death, for example in 216: *'Safe in their Alabaster Chambers'* and 712: *'Because I could not stop for Death'*. In both poems the cycle of human life is presented in terms of nature's cycles, and cycles of space and time.

Nature is seen as positive and secure, even if subject to mutability, in order to heighten the sense of the terrible blank unknown that exists after death. This makes for a wonderfully joyous poem in 214: *'I taste a liquor never brewed'*, where the pleasures and happiness of human life at its best are presented in natural terms through butterflies, flowers and birds. In this way Dickinson harnesses natural images to convey an abstract theme lightly and delicately. Of course, as usual in her poetry, these natural delights are used to contrast with whatever it is that occurs after death.

Nature is also linked to death in another way in the 'dying' poems, 280: *'I felt a Funeral, in my Brain'*, 465: *'I heard a Fly buzz – when I died'* and 1100: *'The last Night that She lived'*. Dickinson secularizes death in all three of the poems; despite the heightened tension and the expectancy, there is no final evidence to support a faith in redemption and salvation. Death is presented as a fact of nature. The point is made clearly in the third of these poems, where the woman's death is described using the natural image of bending towards death as *lightly as a Reed*.

In the 'Poems of Definition', natural images are used in an

attempt to define a state of mind, or a particular experience. In 254: *'"Hope" is the thing with feathers'*, the image of a bird is the nearest she can get to defining a positive experience, but in contrast, in 414: *''Twas like a Maelstrom, with a notch'*, the image is negative as the whirlpool represents the depths of her turbulent distress. Without natural images it would be difficult for Dickinson to handle such abstractions, or to convey them while being able to maintain the lyric form of the poems.

Perhaps one of the most important uses she makes of nature is her constant use of natural images to 'purify' certain of her themes, especially that of human love. Repeatedly she uses natural images to convey sensuous and sensual love. This can be seen in 211: *'Come slowly – Eden!'*, and the device is used in many other poems, for example 213: *'Did the Harebell loose her girdle'*, 249: *'Wild Nights – Wild Nights!'*, 322: *'There came a Day at Summer's Full'* and 446: *'I showed her Heights she never saw'*, with the image of mountaineering. Presenting ideas of a sensual kind in this way works wonderfully for the female poet. There can be no suggestions of coarseness or indelicacy, and no charges of unsuitable content lest they rebound on the accuser's head!

While Dickinson is not a 'nature' poet, she appreciates the beauty of nature; she also has a very keen eye in observing natural detail. She has firm views on the relationship between man and nature, and she makes wide use of natural imagery as a springboard for more abstract ideas and more controversial aspects of her poetry.

Activity

Discuss the ways in which the worlds of nature and man seem inextricably linked in 258: *'There's a certain Slant of light'* and 1068: *'Further in Summer than the Birds'*.

Discussion

It would be a useful exercise to assess how the natural register is combined with the religious register and with the emotional register

of the human psyche to develop meanings in these two poems. In this case, it might be wise to work by moving across the poems as each of the three areas is discussed.

Marriage

Dickinson's poems about marriage fall into two types generally; there is the presentation of conventional marriage, which clearly has abhorrent aspects to Dickinson; then there is the presentation of an idealized, non-conventional marriage which seems to delight the poet.

Conventional marriage is scorned, probably because of the effects on the subservient wife. In 199: *'I'm "wife" – I've finished that'*, the presumably newly married woman speaker ironically gives herself away as she tries to adjust to her new identity. The role of the wife is damned with faint praise, but tellingly the speaker dares not even remember, let alone look back on, her girlhood; the irony of the dramatic monologue is at its best here.

732: *'She rose to His Requirements – dropt'* is more explicitly negative. This marks the diminishing course of the woman's life in a downward movement as the reader moves down the poem. This poem is interesting for the way in which the relationship is presented in almost metaphysical, compressed terms, referring to *Gold*, *Pearl* and *Weed*.

The poet, however, feels happy and confident in a less conventional sort of marriage. There is the promise of marriage in 322: *'There came a Day at Summer's full'* and in 640: *'I cannot live with You'*, both to take place in a life hereafter. The second poem is curious as Dickinson seems calm and accepting in renouncing her love. The renunciation in the first is understandable, as the relationship seems capable of being resumed in heaven. In the second the rejection is permanent, but constitutes a testament to a man loved more than God himself. The only suggestion of distress is the rigid control of form established in the stanzaic structure and the ubiquitous dash, holding tone and thought together as if by a massive effort.

There is real triumph in the jubilant, ecstatic 528: '*Mine – by the Right of the White Election!*' Somewhere among the myriad possible readings of this poem there is a hint about the sort of 'marriage' that Dickinson would accept. The *White Election* has echoes of the wedding dress, of vows made, of dedication. But what is the *Delirious Charter* to which she refers? The reference to *the Sign in the Scarlet prison* implies passion and sexual love, but because there are no precise details this may also relate to poetry and to the role Dickinson has assumed in her life. How curious that the most deliriously joyful poem is about a surreal, spectral marriage, possibly of the artist to her work and her role in life.

Activity

Some critics have suggested that there is a movement in Dickinson's thoughts about love, from meeting to passion to renunciation. How far would you agree?

Discussion

This suggestion raises an interesting issue about Dickinson's poetry. It would seem that she approached all of her topics from a series of different perspectives; sometimes the viewpoints concur and sometimes they totally contrast. What finally emerges is a composite of her views, and it would be impossible to say which is her definitive and final view.

It is possible to arrange the poems in a sequence suggesting a development of thought which seems to be clear and logical, but the development will have been edited by the arranger. This is a perfectly acceptable practice to use in an exam, as long as it is made clear that the arrangement has been deliberately chosen. Either the topic of love or that of marriage would be a good starting point for such an exercise.

War

War is a frequent subject of Dickinson's poetry, probably inspired by the contemporary American Civil War. Poems discussed under the topic of religion on page 156 are relevant here, as are Dickinson's views on God's indifference to man's suffering.

In 67: '*Success is counted sweetest*', there is a negative view of success or defeat in war: each cancels out the other in futility. Yet this early poem is not as harsh as later ones, as the Civil War progresses, and as the poet becomes bolder and more experienced.

In 444: '*It feels a shame to be Alive*', the blame for the futile death of so many young men is laid at the door of society. Money and commerce are at the root of war, as bodies are piled *like Dollars*; there is no true heroism and no just war. The lack of the necessary social bonds is made clear in 1183: '*Step lightly on this narrow spot*'. The anonymous soldiers lie in anonymous graves and society fails to reward those great-hearted heroes. There can be no justification for such a war, either in religious terms or in social terms.

Activity

Would you agree that Dickinson seems to think that war is cruel, pointless and futile?

Discussion

It would seem to be so. War cannot be seen to be justified in human or universal terms in her poetry, again suggesting the failure of a Christian view, according to which war would be seen as redemptive, and the suffering worthwhile in the cause of furthering human destiny. Dickinson seems to suggest that war is not redemptive; having rejected the idea of a Christian scheme of history in her apparently secularized philosophy, war has to be seen as futile and wicked.

Society

On the subject of war, society is heavily criticized, as it is on religion. Sometimes there is satire resting on a lighter basis, and the poetry can be comical, as in the satire on behaviour, and more seriously on morality in 401: '*What Soft – Cherubic*

Creatures'. At first the criticism is gentle, as the women are described as *Plush*; however, when biblical allusions are used in support of the satire, the tone becomes more serious. These women have confused manners and morality; they would reject the disciples and even Jesus for lack of social status.

In 288: *'I'm Nobody! Who are you?'* the focus of the satire turns to a different segment of society, and there is irony this time at the expense of certain politicians. Dickinson addresses 'you' the reader, inviting acceptance of her views.

Her satire extends beyond individuals and she will make criticism about groups in society. In 214: *'I taste a liquor never brewed'* she satirizes the excessive zeal of members of the temperance movement. While she does not attack their principles, there is clearly some mockery of what she might see as obsessive behaviour. Throughout this poem the register picks up their jargon about drinking; it could be that this poem actually supports the temperance movement, however, as the point could be made that with so many joys of life available for free, who needs alcohol to be happy?

There is a tone of criticism mixed with some admiration for technological advance in 585: *'I like to see it lap the Miles'*. The presentation of the 'iron horse' celebrates the power and speed of the locomotive, and her first line avows support. But derogatory references are slipped in; the reader notices that the locomotive is *supercilious* about the shanties of the poor; it sees just a *Pile of Mountains* and not the beauty of nature; and that the countryside is slashed open to allow the train through. In effect there is a suggestion that technological advance comes at a price, and even then the benefits will not be accessible to all.

Social comment in her poetry ranges from the light and teasing, such as that about society women and politicians, to the angry comments on the behaviour of community leaders in times of war. Similarly, the Puritan church is heavily criticized because it has become too much part of the social structure, with too little connection to the principles upon which Christianity was founded.

The 'Poems of Definition'

These are an important category of Dickinson's poetry because they are often her most imaginative poems. It is generally accepted that such poems are autobiographical and testify to the mental trauma she suffered throughout her life, and which may finally have killed her. It is in these poems that her quest for identity and self-knowledge is at its clearest. To come to terms with herself she had to define and try to understand all her experiences. In these dynamic poems, the 'it' of the poem is always elusive; the poems work by making analogies or by a negative approach that explains what something is not.

In 254: '*"Hope" is the thing with feathers*', the tone is as light as a bird. This positive poem sustains the analogy throughout the poem, so that although the abstract experience of *Hope* cannot be defined, it can be understood by readers. This poem differs from others of this category which Dickinson seems to write after dreadful suffering. In 414: '*'Twas like a Maelstrom, with a notch*', violent images drawn from nature are used to suggest dreadful psychological trauma. The pain seems to be less evident in 341: '*After great pain, a formal feeling comes*'; it is apparent that the speaker has survived a trauma, but the feelings remaining are not positive. Feeling wretched, like a prisoner coming out of prison, the speaker is still unsure whether it was worth surviving.

Evidently, 510: '*It was not Death, for I stood up*', was written in a similar mood. Time and space count for nothing as the speaker does not know how to even begin describing the trauma. This time Dickinson uses double devices: she proceeds by both analogy and opposition. It was not frost, but it certainly felt like it; on the other hand, it cannot have been fire, although it felt like being caught in extreme heat. The complexity of the devices does suggest the complexity of the suffering.

Poems of psychological experiences and personal values

Some readers see poems such as 512: '*The Soul has Bandaged moments*' as a 'Poem of Definition', but it seems unlike these in many ways. Whereas the true 'Poems of Definition' are evidence of an effort to define an unnameable experience, this poem and others like it testify to attitudes and values which Dickinson feels are assured. Again, it is generally accepted that this type of poem is autobiographical.

In the curious 670: '*One need not be a Chamber – to be Haunted*', the anguished tone of the earlier category of poems is picked up. The speaker describes mental trauma in a terrifying account of suffering as the dangers within the mind are presented in Gothic terms. Dickinson makes wonderful use of the Gothic tradition and the analogy seems absolutely just and appropriate.

In 303: '*The Soul selects her own Society*', the tone changes from the anguish of many of the former poems to one of joy and satisfaction in an account of the way a pattern in the human spirit is defined. The tone is confident. The *Soul* has to make a choice of *One* from the *divine Majority*, but there is a feeling that this is natural and non-traumatic. What exactly had to be chosen remains obscure; it might be the choice of writing poetry as the role in life, or the choice of a lover (physical or spiritual). Again the ambiguity generates many levels of meaning. But the point of the poem is that this choice has to be made and the speaker is happy making it.

In another poem a choice is the central focus, but in 747: '*It dropped so low – in my Regard*' the choice was evidently not a sound one. This is very close to being a 'Poem of Definition' as there is an *It* in the poem which remains undefined. The reader is left to wonder whether it was a choice about love, companionship, or religion – again ambiguity, analogy and compression create a wide spectrum of meanings. But what is clearly evident in the poem is the self-analysis which implies a search for self-knowledge, as the speaker queries her own earlier misjudgement. The tone is not anguished, merely self-critical.

In 512: *'The Soul has Bandaged moments'*, there is an explanation of what seems at first to be obscure. The analogy of the bandages is persuasive and acceptable as an account of the poet's values – the image representing restriction is wonderfully apt, and the poem does something to reveal how the creative impulses work within the writer herself. The experience of horror which dominated several of the former poems is alleviated here, as periods of suffering are alternated with periods of great joy and creativity.

Presumably 754: *'My Life had stood – a Loaded Gun'* similarly defines something of the poet's values if it is read as autobiographical. The poem is cast as a riddle in some ways. Perhaps words are seen as bullets; in an age when war has damaged society so greatly, images of warfare have become part of the natural vocabulary of a writer. Perhaps it is safest to assume that on one level of meaning there are autobiographical roots, but that these are deeply embedded in other issues.

The speaker's values are again defined in 657: *'I dwell in Possibility'*, but this time less obscurely. Clearly the subject matter of the poem is again about a choice, but this choice has been made successfully and apparently wisely. The tone of the poem is confident as the value of being a poet is clear and undoubted. This time, perhaps, it is the reader who feels saddened because of the *narrow* life the poet has opted for in self-imposed isolation from human company.

In 327: *'Before I got my eye put out'*, the implications of this choice can be seen to be extended. Despite the very Gothic-sounding title, this poem is not at all horrific or anguished. In the course of the poem it becomes clear that the blinding was not only metaphorical, but was also made out of choice. The choice made might at first glance seem restricting, but in fact offers the speaker the world. Strangely, the poem again might leave the reader feeling slightly saddened for the isolated speaker; the image of the poet at the window *with just my soul/Upon the Window pane* is deeply moving.

Activity

The 'Poems of Definition' and poems which define experience and personal values are important in the poetry of Emily Dickinson. What might readers think is significant about them?

Discussion

As in the war poems, these poems are extremely significant because they are presented as universal rather than purely personal experiences. They are in a sense handed over to the reader as problems that all may experience. The poet generally keeps the 'I' out of the poem so that there is no subjectivity, and a powerful presentation is offered which testifies to her grasp of poetic forms and movements.

The poet exploits the Romantic genre and the Gothic genre as well as the metaphysical tradition; images are drawn from nature, from psychology and from science. Philosophies offered include the nihilist, the theological, the existentialist and that of the stoic, who will endure much. Accordingly there is a huge range of tone, from ecstatic through contentedness to despair.

There is evidence of a wonderful fusion of many things in her poetry, and interestingly, it is a fusion she searches for in each poem. The point about Dickinson's handling of traditions from many different periods is that she is able to ensure a relevance to all readers.

Poetry about writing poetry

In some poems the issues that result from choosing the role of poet, and problems that arise in the course of writing poetry, are considered, as though Dickinson is recording the working through of her discoveries or her difficulties. Generally this category of poems is written in a light mood, as is evident in 657: '*I dwell in Possibility*'.

Dickinson was aware of having something to offer to others, as is clear in 441: '*This is my letter to the World*'. It is generally assumed that this poem is autobiographical, although she takes some liberties with the literal truth. Her poems were well received when she sent them out, and 986: '*A narrow Fellow in the Grass*' was printed on the cover of *The Springfield Republican*. However, she was not known to the world at large, which may have been saddening and frustrating. It is impossible perhaps for a reader to avoid the interpretation that this is a personal plea to her *countrymen* some time in the future to think *tenderly* of her quality as a poet. In simple language, she makes a simple plea.

In a way this poem complements 709: '*Publication – is the Auction*'. Reading the poems side by side, it is easy to understand why her own world knew so little of Dickinson. But again, this poem is universal as well as personal. All artists know the anguish of putting a price on something so precious as a creation of their own. The argument she rehearses will be rehearsed evermore: how can you put a price on a talent given by God? Many would agree that the marketplace degrades the *Human Spirit*. This is obviously the working out of a difficult decision, but this poem holds validity for each new generation of artists facing the same challenge. Through its parody of the jargon of commerce and trade, the poem appeals for approval for the decision made.

Some explanation of the process of writing poetry is offered in the cryptic 1138: '*A Spider sewed at Night*'. Here some account is given of the relationship of the artist to society. How, where and when does a poet actually write? This poem offers some clues. The image that has now become traditional of the artist working in his or her garret is presented here. The image of the night may be suggesting many things at once. There is the idea of social isolation, but at the same time the darkness summons up the idea of the blindness of the true prophet illuminated by the inner light of vision. The poem rests on contrasts, and the opposing whiteness again is suggestive of many meanings, including that of heavenly light and purity. Dickinson uses both metaphysical (the image of the spider and his physiognomy) and classical elements (that of spinning) to create a poem about the vision and integrity of the poet, among other things. No sense of anxiety is evident in this reading.

There is also no anxiety when the speaker explains the roots of poetry in 741: '*Drama's Vitallest Expression is the Common Day*'. Here the sources of poetry are explained as coming to the poet from ordinary life. There is a neat play on the idea of drama in the theatre and drama in everyday life: *Hamlet* and *Romeo and Juliet* were in any case based on how real human beings behave. Perhaps the poet is not so isolated after all, as there must be a fully populated world in his or her head. Furthermore, the speaker claims, this is not a limited topic, because unlike theatres, the human drama can never be closed down. The tone is confident and rather playful here.

The poems that perhaps most of all celebrate her choice of role, and which again most readers believe are autobiographical, are 528: '*Mine – by the Right of the White Election!*' and 1072: '*Title divine – is mine!*'. The first thing to note is that of course these poems carry multiple meanings; they could be related to love, or a type of marriage, as well as to the vocation of the poet. In the first, the speaker is jubilant about the *Delirious Charter* that has been given and signed. If this is taken as being about poetry, there might be a reference in the *Grave's Repeal* to literary immortality. The speaker suggests that long after her death she will be famed for her poetry; this is one of the moments where there seems to be a positive and pleasurable philosophy of life.

In the second poem the reference to *Calvary* and the words related to the register of love and marriage stand out clearly; however, it is also possible that the *Title divine* is in fact that of the poet/visionary, who sometimes suffers for his or her art. It is possible that the speaker is addressing this poem to the audience as a demonstration of the art of poetry writing; hence the last two lines, *Stroking the Melody – /Is* this *– the way?* might feasibly be directed to the reader as a request for approval for the poem, with its rhythm or *Melody*.

Most of these issues seem to be combined in 1129: '*Tell all the Truth but tell it slant*'. This time the speaker refers to the philosophy behind the writing, and explains the ethos of the speaker generally. The word *slant* is a metaphor borrowed from the language of poetry itself; it is a half-rhyme, which looks as though it rhymes, but does not. The message is one of compassion: too much horror will be too much for humans to bear (as in the war poetry). The matter of *slant* reporting might well apply to concerns about religion, where since there is no certainty, there has to be 'slanted' evidence. As far as the love poetry is concerned, passionate love has to be reported in encoded or *slant* ways. Dickinson clearly had no intention of allowing anyone into her confidence over her possible love affairs.

Some readers might feel that the argument for *Success in Circuit*, in revealing poetic truths to readers referred to as *Children*, is simply patronizing. It seems more likely that it was felt to be wiser not to fully disclose all her disillusionment about both church and state and that the motive is compassionate. Finally, of course, there is the matter of anonymity; the truths had to be *slant* so that they were distanced from the author – perhaps for his or her own safety as well as for privacy.

Language and style

There are certain characteristics of Dickinson's style that are the hallmarks of her writing, and are crucial to the generation of meanings. The secularization of religious language and tropes is one of these dominant features. It is evident in poems on any topic; in 322: '*There came a Day at Summer's full*', ritual and sacramental language elevates the presentation of a love relationship, and in her nature poems (as in 1068: '*Further in Summer than the Birds*') this has the effect of solemnizing a moment in the natural world to create the mood for a pensive meditation on the condition of mankind.

A second characteristic is the way in which she proceeds by setting up analogies or oppositions to help define an experience or situation, or to crystallize the views offered to the reader. In 510: '*It was not Death, for I stood up*', both devices are used to present a complex experience. It is not a matter of reconciling polarized positions; it is enough to state them and let the reader do the rest. In fact the oppositions are seldom reconciled, and at times create a paradox, as in 585: *'I like to see it lap the Miles'* and differently in 640: *'I cannot live with You'*. This leads inevitably into the use of mixed registers within a poem to achieve similar effects.

Another important technique, especially valuable in the 'Poems of Definition', is the assigning of a concrete form to an abstract experience. For example, hope is represented by a bird, trauma is seen as a maelstrom, and the choice of the role of poet is made physical by the analogy of having an eye put out. This also occurs in other types of poetry, such as the harebell loosing her girdle, perhaps to indicate loss of virginity. Related to this, Dickinson often presents abstract ideas in very sensuous ways, as in the image of the bee entering a flower to symbolize achieving something long desired; throughout her poetry, the reader is engaged by a mass of sensuous experience, as in 258: *'There's a certain Slant of light'*.

Dickinson is rightly famed for the effectiveness of her often startling opening lines; she achieves a variety of effects though this, but of course the primary purpose is to make sure that the reader feels compelled to continue reading the poem. Opening lines can shock by their apparent illogicality, as in 280: *'I felt a Funeral, in my Brain'*, or may be seductively inviting: *Wild Nights – Wild Nights!* Sometimes the poet appears to directly challenge the reader: *I'm Nobody! Who are you?*; or there may be a confessional, personal note: *In Winter in my Room*. At times the opening line is cryptic and strange (*A Spider sewed at Night*) or seems to invite an intellectual response (*This World is not Conclusion*). Punctuation is always purposeful, as in *She rose to His Requirement – dropt*, where the combination of the dash and final word *dropt*, in clear opposition to the earlier *rose*, force the reader into a pause.

Compression is a vital element of Dickinson's style, allowing for the generation of multiple meanings. The reader can group and regroup words as a result. This is wonderfully evident in the key line of 1072: *'Title divine – is mine!'* where three single words

Born – Bridalled – Shrouded declare the entire life story of a married woman.

Compression is movingly effective in 327: '*Before I got my eye put out*', where the last stanza begins *So safer – guess – with just my soul/Upon the Window pane*. Here there is grammatical incompleteness as there is no verb, but this makes 'space' for the reader to imagine the rest.

Metaphysical compression through the use of an image or conceit has been discussed earlier (page 149). The image in 1138: '*A Spider sewed at Night*' is a fine example of imagery that might be benign or terrifying. Another method of creating compression is through her use of metonyms, such as the *Flag* in 67: '*Success is counted sweetest*' and 1183: '*Step lightly on this narrow spot*', used as a shorthand to represent the men fighting in war. Elsewhere, synecdoche achieves great compression, as in 211: '*Come slowly – Eden!*' where the speaker becomes reduced to just a pair of lips, or in 322: '*There came a Day at Summer's full*' where the separated lovers become simply hands at first and then vanishing faces.

Frequently there are unusual usages of words to make the reader think; this is evident in poems such as 1068: '*Further in Summer than the Birds*', where the first word opens up several readings, and the strange word *Antiquest* creates the same effect.

These devices are all part of Dickinson's quiet but firm rebellion against traditional forms, and a new form of poetic language emerges through stripping off conventional connotations and even denotations. A verb may become a noun and vice versa, yet the language is always highly evocative, if almost impossible to paraphrase at times, and layers of meaning are created.

Her use of concrete imagery is often the key to achieving effects; a soul's time of painful constriction is seen as *Bandaged*; a railway locomotive becomes the 'iron horse'; and perhaps most shockingly of all a speaker's life becomes a *Loaded Gun*. Over and over again the reader is forced to look afresh at once-familiar language which becomes revitalized. This makes for a strenuous reading experience as the reader is constantly forced to work in partnership with the author to reach meanings.

Humour in Dickinson's poetry

Dickinson had a keen sense of humour which was often waspish. There is plenty of evidence of this in her letters, and it comes out in her poetry as well. It ranges from delightfully robust humour to very dark irony used in a non-humorous way.

The most exuberant of her poems is probably 214: '*I taste a liquor never brewed*', where Dickinson celebrates the sheer joy of life. She playfully uses the language of the temperance movement to suggest the pleasure of the *little Tippler*, drunk on the delight of earthly existence. Images drawn from nature serve to convince the reader of the carefree happiness portrayed. The use of common metre introduces a celebratory tone, and this joyous poem seems to aim to persuade the reader to share in its joy. Surely, if even the *Seraphs* are so entranced that they *swing their snowy Hats*, and if even the *Saints* are captivated, then so will the reader be.

A sense of fun evident is also in other poems, such as 79: '*Going to Heaven!*'. This is a different type of humour as the reader sees the tone, that of a young child at first, change. The language is endearing, indicating the naivety of imagining a trip to heaven as a sort of special day out, and thinking about what to wear. But in this dramatic monologue there is irony as the reader watches the implications dawn on the speaker, who suddenly rejects the idea of death and heaven at the beginning of the third stanza.

There is a similar sense of fun in 986: '*A narrow Fellow in the Grass*', with the internal rhyme of the first line sounding playful and informal. This is similar to 585: '*I like to see it lap the Miles*', which is also cast in the form of a riddle; the image of the iron horse is amusing, but in both poems the humour serves to underline the fact that both snake and locomotive are capable of bringing danger. Both need to be treated with caution.

Perhaps it is the use of the gentle natural metaphors in 211: '*Come slowly – Eden!*' and 213: '*Did the Harebell loose her girdle*' which make both poems seem rather playful; however, as with the previous three poems the humour is there perhaps to soften the blow, as Dickinson in both cases offers moral fables about the dangers inherent when long-held desires are achieved.

The assertive way the reader is challenged in 288: *'I'm Nobody! Who are you?'* is humorous; this is certainly attention-grabbing. There are some moments of witty, waspish humour in 1072: *'Title divine – is mine!'* and 1670: *'In Winter in my Room'*. In the first, Dickinson celebrates her life freed from conventional forms of marriage. She would seem to think that this institution is very damaging for women, but there is some humour here. Talking of betrothal, the poet comments that she will be free from *the swoon/God sends us Women*. This is a jibe both at feminine emotional excess, and at the God who appears to send nothing but problems. The second poem is amusing throughout; the poet makes a witty aside to the reader with *And worms presume*. Probably at some level of meaning Dickinson considers the male will to dominance in this poem, and these three words sum up her ridicule of such attitudes. The whole of this poem could be a 'winter's tale' to tease her readers.

Another aspect of Dickinson's humour lies in her satire. The warning to society in 585: *'I like to see it lap the Miles'* has already been noted, and 401: *'What Soft – Cherubic Creatures'* is another warning to women. The tone is witty; women are compared to *Plush* in a tone of contempt, and a *Star*, suggesting frigidity. But yet again, the poem ends on a serious note warning about misjudgements.

The poems are shot through with irony, astutely set up for example in the dense first line of 732: *'She rose to His Requirement – dropt'*. As has been noted before, the contrast between *rose* and *dropt* summarizes the central theme of the poem. Not all the humour is positive. There is the black humour of 465: *'I heard a Fly buzz – when I died'*. It is a characteristic of Dickinson's humour that it varies from joyful and playful to darker tones, but always serves to remind the reader of larger and usually darker ideas.

Punctuation

Throughout her poetry Dickinson makes use of four notable methods of punctuation: capitalization, dashes, exclamation marks and question marks. Of these the first is troublesome. Capitalization is not always a reliable guide to finding significances and meanings, as she appears to have been erratic and non-systematic in using it. Some readers suggest that she is following a Germanic form by capitalizing nouns, but generally it is agreed that it is not wise to set too much store by its use.

Sometimes capitalization seems to be used to stress important words, as in 501: '*This World is not Conclusion*' or 732: '*She rose to His Requirement – dropt*'. But at other times the usage seems to be more arbitrary, as in the two versions of 216: '*Safe in their Alabaster Chambers*'. The first reads *Rafter of satin,/And Roof of stone*. In the second version Dickinson capitalizes *Satin* and *Stone*. In 214: '*I taste a liquor never brewed*', there is no capitalization in the first line, but in the body of the poem one line reads *When Butterflies – renounce their 'drams'*. Why should *Butterflies* be capitalized, when the poem plays on the analogy of drinking?

The dash is everywhere in Dickinson's poetry and seems to be very important to her in defining meaning. She uses it to control the pace of a poem and determine mood and tone. Frequently she uses the dash to deny closure to a poem, as in 712: '*Because I could not stop for Death*'. The dash at the end of the poem is quite logical, as the speaker has no knowledge of anything after death, so there could not be closure. In 986: '*A narrow Fellow in the Grass*', the final dash seems to be used to suggest that the danger of confronting a snake will occur over and over again.

Sometimes she uses the dash to slow down a line, as in 657: '*I dwell in Possibility*', which has the leisurely line *Superior – for Doors* –, which catches the expansiveness of the poet's world. But dashes used in lines such as *Born – Bridalled – Shrouded* – (in 1072: '*Title divine – is mine!*') do not seem leisurely at all; instead they fall heavily like a funeral toll; the effect depends on the alliteration, images and context.

Sometimes the dash builds up tension, as in 280: *'I felt a Funeral, in my Brain'* with the startling line *Kept treading – treading – till it seemed*; here, it works in combination with the use of repetition.

At other times the dash is used to create a montage of expansive thought, as in 327: *'Before I got my eye put out'* with the joyous lines: *The Meadows – mine –/The Mountains – mine – /All Forests – Stintless Stars –*. Here the dash reinforces the impression of vastness. The dash can also be used to cut across and vary the metre, as in the last quotation.

The use of exclamation marks is bound to affect the tone and mood of the poem, as clearly a sense of excitement or shock will be created. *Mine – by the Right of the White Election!* is obviously jubilant in tone; in *Wild Nights – Wild Nights!* there is a sense of sexual excitement. At times exclamations are used to challenge the reader: *I'm Nobody! Who are you?* Here it works in close combination with the question mark. Inevitably the question mark is used to challenge the reader to think and engage closely with the poem.

In Dickinson's hands all these devices become versatile tools for enlivening the poetry, making it new, shocking and challenging.

Rhythm

Dickinson uses a variety of devices to vary the pace of her poetry, including assonance, consonance, alliteration and enjambment, where the sense flows through from stanza to stanza. (All of these terms are explained in the Glossary on page 196.) In most of her poetry she uses a simple common metre, which is the rhythm of many of the hymns with which she was brought up, and is also the rhythm of the ballad form. However, to vary the rhythm and pace she uses the dash, as discussed above, and other methods included varying line lengths, as in 585: *'I like to see it lap the Miles'*. Flexible and varied rhyme schemes are also used, and will be considered in the next section.

Common metre form consists of an eight-syllable line followed by a six-syllable line, with mostly iambic stress patterns, and a rhyme scheme usually *abab* or *abcb*. It is used in many English hymns. Here is an example (the 'ie' of the word *Holiest* in the first line is elided to make the word two syllables):

> Praise to the Holiest in the height
> And in the depth be praise!
> In all his words most wonderful,
> Most sure in all his ways! (John Henry Newman)

Dickinson often varies the metre a little, and uses half-rhyme, for example. Elsewhere she will temporarily change the metre but resume the common metre after she has created the effect she needs. A typical example would be 585: *'I like to see it lap the Miles'*. The first stanza is straightforward common metre, with half-rhymes and alliteration on 'l' and 'k' in the first lines to create an appropriate sound effect:

> I like to see it lap the Miles –
> And lick the Valleys up –
> And stop to feed itself at Tanks –
> And then – prodigious step

But the third stanza describes the slowing of the train as it crawls on a track just wide enough to take it:

> To fit its Ribs
> And crawl between
> Complaining all the while
> In horrid – hooting stanza –
> Then chase itself down Hill –

The lines of this stanza are shortened to represent the slowing of the locomotive, but lines 3 and 5 retain the six-syllable pattern, and in the final stanza common metre is used once more.

Activity

Analyse Dickinson's use of metre in 986: '*A narrow Fellow in the Grass*'.

Discussion

Dickinson plays with the metre after the first two stanzas of this poem, and again, it is the six-syllable line that keeps a basic rhythm going throughout the poem.

Rhyme

Dickinson uses a variety of types of rhyme in her poetry: masculine rhyme, feminine rhyme, half-rhyme and internal rhyme, and it is always used purposefully to reinforce or even to extend meanings. In 986: '*A narrow Fellow in the Grass*', the internal rhyme of the first line introduces a light-hearted note. On the other hand, full masculine rhyme is always forceful and creates a variety of effects, especially when used at the end of a poem. At the end of 1551: '*Those – dying then*', the masculine rhyme of *small/all* draws the poem to a close on what appears to be a note of contempt. After the joy and exuberance of 214: '*I taste a liquor never brewed*', the poem ends with the strong masculine rhyme of *run/Sun*, which seems most appropriate.

At other times Dickinson uses a carefully plotted rhyme scheme to extend the meaning of a poem. In the lines *Title divine – is mine/The Wife – without the Sign!* her use of rhyme is complex. She combines the internal rhyme on *divine* with the full masculine rhyme *Sign* and also, through assonance, with *Wife*. This is followed by the feminine rhyme at *Calvary* (line 4), along with an internal rhyme in *Degree* (line 3). What results is a balance between feminine and masculine, internal and full rhymes, which could be said to support one of the meanings of this poem.

There is a similar usage in 249: '*Wild Nights – Wild Nights!*'. Here the feminine rhyme of *luxury* (line 4) might suggest the uncertainty of the speaker, but this combines with the masculine rhyme of *thee/be* (lines 2/3), which suggests some sort of emotional certainty, and taken together the combination of masculine/feminine rhyme might suggest a coming together of the sexes, which is represented in one layer of meaning in the poem.

A mixture of rhymes is also evident in 1138: '*A Spider sewed at Night*'; here the initial *Night/White/Light* rhymes enforce the sense of the masculine power of the spider. However, there is a possibility that this poem might be about creativity, which would include a female author, and the rhyme scheme yields in support of this idea to the feminine half-rhymes of *Immortality/Strategy/Physiognomy*.

In 1068: '*Further in Summer than the Birds*', the rhymes are erratic; there is full masculine rhyme in the first stanza, perhaps to capture the sense of communion amongst the insects, and the rhymes of *low* (line 10) and *Glow* (line 14) work across two stanzas. Interestingly this also pulls in the half-rhyme *now* of the last line. Perhaps the intermittent rhymes suggest the touch of the ghostly finger of death in the midst of life.

Dickinson's rhyme schemes can be complex and varied, sometimes insistent, sometimes barely there. Often they work to combat the regularity of common metre. In 249: '*Wild Nights – Wild Nights!*' the rich rhyme scheme including masculine, feminine, half-rhyme, internal rhyme and assonance promotes the tone of the speaking voice and complements the rhythm.

In 501: '*This World is not Conclusion*' there is little rhyme, as if to suggest that opposing philosophies cannot be harnessed together successfully.

A final comment on Dickinson's use of language, rhyme and metre would be: do not expect anything regular; in her poetry there is always something unexpected.

Critical history

Dickinson was little known during her lifetime beyond her own area of New England. About a dozen poems had been printed and about 500 were sent to friends, some of which were read aloud at reading groups and shared in other ways. It was a shock to most people when over a thousand poems were discovered in a drawer after her death by her sister Lavinia.

The two people who took an immediate interest in editing her poetry were her lifelong friend Thomas Higginson and the mistress of her brother, Mabel Loomis Todd, a shrewd woman formerly the wife of a university professor. They issued the first edition of her poems in 1890, and the attendant publicity described Dickinson as a disturbed social recluse, dressed in white, mysterious and strange.

Mabel Loomis Todd, Dickinson's first editor

On the other side of her family her niece Martha Dickinson Bianchi had control of some of the poems that Lavinia gave her (there was to be a dreadful 'war' about the ownership of the poems), and in 1914 issued another edition of the poems called *The Single Hound*; evidently she was not a good editor and took liberties with the poems, changing lines here and there; however, some readers suggest that this anticipates the line of enquiry of the later deconstructionist theories. In Bianchi's publicity she presented Dickinson as all hearts and roses, feelings and passion, which was as misleading as the earlier idea. However, the still limited number of poems in the public domain had begun to make an impression.

Several further editions appeared as new poems were discovered, and some of the letters were published. But her reputation did not really advance until the 1930s, when Amy Lowell included Dickinson's poetry in her lectures. Lowell was particularly impressed by the compression of the images, which fused emotion and intellect in way that was seen as Imagist. Then Yvor Winters, a member of the 'New Critics' school of criticism, promoted her writing. This group was united against what they saw as the chaos induced by Marxism in society, and focusing closely on the text itself, they saw in her poetry a wealth of cultural values.

Major recognition came in 1945 after Todd's edition of her poems, *Bolts of Melody* (withheld from publication until after Martha Bianchi's death) was published. After the changes in society brought about by two world wars, mass unemployment and economic depression, there was a need for poetry capable of speaking to the new age. Dickinson's revolutionary use of language was superbly suited to this. Family feuds over her texts were finally ended and the manuscripts were placed at Boston Public Library, Amherst College Library and the Houghton Library at Harvard University.

In 1955 Thomas H. Johnson produced the first full, three-volume edition of Dickinson's poems, although some were still being recovered; this remains the standard edition of her work. Three years later he published the letters, and in 1960 a huge variorum edition showing all the versions of her poems was also published. In 1981 R.W. Franklin published his complete edition of her poems, *The Manuscript Books of Emily Dickinson*. Richard Sewell's *The Life of Emily Dickinson* was published in 1974 and remains the classic two-volume biography. In 1951 the first scholarly critical book appeared, *Emily Dickinson* by Richard Chase, for the 'American Men of Letters' series. It was thoroughly researched, though now seems a little dated. It focuses on the themes of the poetry.

Dickinson is now highly regarded as a leading American poet, appreciated by critics from many different backgrounds. Some critics take a specific interest in linguistics, and these include Cristanne Miller's *Emily Dickinson: A Poet's Grammar*; other approaches include the deconstructive approach of Helen McNeil's *Emily Dickinson.* Margaret Homans offers a study of this area in *Bearing the Word: Language and Female Experience in Nineteenth-Century Women's Writing*, in which she also considers the poet as a feminist writer as does Suzanne Juhasz in *Feminist Critics Read Emily Dickinson.*

Feminism is considered in many of the poet's contexts including her rebellion against male-oriented poetic forms. In Joanne Feir Diehl's *Dickinson and the Romantic Imagination*, there is an argument for Dickinson as a subverter of the Romantic tradition, while Sandra M. Gilbert and Susan Gubar place her firmly in the British tradition in *The Madwoman in the Attic: The Woman Writer and the Nineteenth-Century Literary Imagination.*

Daneen Wardrop investigates her links with the Gothic tradition in *Emily Dickinson's Gothic: Goblin with a Gauge.* Dickinson lived very much in her own society and in her own mind, and this is developed in Suzanne Juhasz's explorative text *The Undiscovered Continent: Emily Dickinson and the Space of the Mind.* Mary Loeffelholz offers a psychoanalytical approach in *Dickinson and the Boundaries of Feminist Theory.*

The poems, especially the dramatic monologues, are wonderful to read aloud, and Elizabeth Phillips studies this aspect of the poetry in her book *Emily Dickinson: Personae and Performance.* The contexts of Dickinson's poetry are important to the student of today, and Barton Levi St Armand offers a study of literary contexts in *Emily Dickinson and Her Culture: The Soul's Society.*

The recent interest in textuality, a theory in which the manuscript itself is as important as the words on the page, is reflected in Susan Howe's *The Birthmark: Unsettling the Wilderness in American Literary History*.

With the high seriousness of her purposes for herself, for women generally and for all of society, it is easy to overlook Dickinson's sense of humour; there is an entertaining and interesting study of this in *Comic Power in Emily Dickinson* by Suzanne Juhasz, Cristanne Miller and Martha Nell Smith.

Finally, an accessible and useful compendium of contextual aspects of her work can be found in two handy books: *A Historical Guide to Emily Dickinson*, edited by Vivian R. Pollak, offers such contexts as those of war, politics and language, and *The Cambridge Companion to Emily Dickinson*, edited by Wendy Martin, offers considerations of various contexts such as class, gender, and culture. These last two are ideal introductory books for a student coming afresh to the poetry of Emily Dickinson.

Essay Questions

1 Compare the ways in which modern readers might respond to '*Safe in their Alabaster Chambers*' (both versions), and '*Wild Nights – Wild Nights!*' with the ways in which readers of Emily Dickinson's time might have responded.

2 How would you react to the comment that it is only her language which continues to interest readers in the poetry of Emily Dickinson?

3 *I thought that nature was enough/Till Human nature came.* With reference to at least **three** poems from this selection, discuss Emily Dickinson's response to nature.

4 'The only marriage which Emily Dickinson would have tolerated would have been a highly unconventional marriage.' Using a selection of her poetry as evidence, say how far you agree with this comment.

5 Discuss the different types of love which Emily Dickinson presents in her poetry. You should **either** look at **two** poems in detail, **or** range more widely through her poems.

6 'God is dead' (Nietzsche). How far do you think that Emily Dickinson shares this viewpoint? You should include at least **three** poems in your answer.

7 'It is the dramatic openings which are the hallmark of Emily Dickinson's poetry'. How far do you agree with this judgement?

8 Do you think that in Emily Dickinson's poetry fear of men and of sexuality is presented? You should include at least **three** poems in your response.

9 What do you make of Emily Dickinson's views on religion?

10 'She saw immortality as an extension of earthly joys.' Beginning with '*There came a Day at Summer's full*', explain how you respond to this comment.

11 Many critics have suggested that a restrained tension gives the poems their vitality. How do you react to this comment?

12 How does Emily Dickinson present the experience of being a woman in the nineteenth century? Begin with '*She rose to His Requirement – dropt*'.

13 How significant is the problem of mental trauma in the poetry of Emily Dickinson? You should include at least **three** poems in your response.

14 'The "Poems of Definition" actually fail to define.' How far do you agree with this comment, and does it matter if no definition is presented?

15 What does Emily Dickinson have to say about the experience of being a poet? Begin with '*I dwell in Possibility*' and go on to consider **two** or **three** more poems.

16 Compare the attitude to war which Emily Dickinson presents in '*Those – dying then*' and **two** or **three** other poems.

17 How effective is Dickinson's use of the Gothic genre to create effects? Consider closely '*One need not be a Chamber – to be Haunted*' and **one** other poem in detail, **or** you may include a range of other poems if you wish.

18 Write about **three** or **four** poems which you have found to be moving, explaining your response to them.

19 Discuss the range of personae presented in the dramatic monologues, including at least **three** poems in your answer.

20 What impression does Emily Dickinson present of life in nineteenth-century America?

21 What do you consider to be the most important characteristics of Emily Dickinson's poetry?

22 Discuss the ways in which Emily Dickinson has presented sexual love in her poetry. You should consider at least **three** poems in your answer.

23 'Emily Dickinson was obsessed with martyrdom.' How do you respond to this idea, and to the ways in which martyrdom is presented in her poetry?

24 What do you think are the typical characteristics of Emily Dickinson's poetry?

25 Discuss Emily Dickinson's skill in making her monologues dramatic. You should begin with '*Because I could not stop for Death*' and go on to consider at least **two** further poems.

26 Consider how '*I heard a Fly buzz – when I died*' and ''*Twas like a Maelstrom, with a notch*' are typical of Emily Dickinson's poetry. You should range more widely in your response.

27 If you were asked to choose **three** poems from this selection as your favourite poems, which would you select and why?

28 In what ways is Emily Dickinson effective in presenting changing moods in her poetry?

29 Write about the humour in Emily Dickinson's poetry.

30 'Emily Dickinson is a compassionate poet who is concerned for the well-being of her fellow men.' Discussing at least **three** poems from this selection, explain how you respond to this idea.

Chronology

Emily Dickinson's life

1829 Austin, Emily Dickinson's brother, born
1830 10 December: Emily Dickinson born at Amherst, Massachusetts, New England; the family move into 'The Homestead' to live with her grandfather
1833 Lavinia, Emily Dickinson's sister, born
1838 Edward Dickinson, Emily's father, begins a two-year term in the Massachusetts legislature
1840 The Dickinson family move into a spacious wooden house on Pleasant Street; Dickinson enrols at Amherst Academy
1842 Edward Dickinson re-elected for a second term in the Massachusetts Legislature
1844 Dickinson visits her Aunt Lavinia in Boston
1847 After completing her education at Amherst Academy, Dickinson goes on to Mount Holyoke Female Seminary
1848 Dickinson leaves the seminary after completing just one year of the two-year course
1849 A social year for Dickinson in which she records that she had 'fun'; Dickinson sends a comic valentine in the form of a poem to William Cowper Dickinson at Amherst College
1850 Benjamin Franklin Newton, one of her father's clerks, gives Dickinson a copy of Ralph Waldo Emerson's poetry; she would call him her 'tutor'
1852 Dickinson sends a love letter to Susan Huntington Gilbert
1853 Benjamin Franklin Newton dies unexpectedly; Austin Dickinson goes up to Harvard Law School and becomes engaged to Sue Gilbert; Dickinson runs away from the opening of the great railway link to Amherst
1854 Dickinson and Sue Gilbert quarrel; Sue goes away for seven months
1855 Dickinson and her sister Lavinia spend several weeks in Washington. On the return journey Dickinson meets

Reverend Charles Wadsworth; the Dickinson family move into the spacious family house 'The Homestead' which her grandfather had built and then lost through bankruptcy; Dickinson's mother becomes invalided and she nurses her

1856 Sue Gilbert marries Austin Dickinson

1857 A 'lost' year of Dickinson's life; virtually no records kept

1858 Dickinson begins to sew her poems into 'fascicles'; the first of her 'Master' letters is written, followed by two others in 1861 and 1862; she comments on how much she is enjoying society at Austin's and Sue's home

1860 Reverend Charles Wadsworth visits Dickinson; she writes '*There came a Day at Summer's full*'; after this year her withdrawal from society begins after visiting her friend Eliza Coleman at Middletown

1861 Sue and Austin Dickinson's first child is born; Emily experiences her 'terror' in September; her period of great poetic output begins

1862 After reading an article in the *Atlantic Monthly*, Dickinson sends some poems to Thomas Higginson; Reverend Charles Wadsworth leaves to take up his new ministry at San Francisco, California

1863 Dickinson writes or copies out 300 of her poems

1864 Dickinson goes to Boston for specialist eye treatment; her brother Austin is drafted into the army but buys his way out

1865 Dickinson returns to Boston for seven months more of eye treatment

1866 '*A narrow fellow in the Grass*' is printed on the cover of *The Springfield Republican*

1869 Thomas Higginson asks Emily Dickinson to visit him in Boston; she refuses, saying that she would not cross her father's ground 'for any house or town'

1870 Thomas Higginson visits Dickinson

1874 Dickinson's father dies in June of a heart attack while attending the legislature

1875 Dickinson's mother suffers a major stroke on the anniversary of her husband's death
1878 Dickinson begins a relationship with Judge Otis Lord, which blossoms into a proposal which she declines
1881 Mabel Loomis Todd begins to record details of her time with the Dickinson family
1882 Dickinson's mother dies
1883 Gilbert, Dickinson's beloved nephew, dies
1884 Otis Lord, one of Dickinson's suitors, dies
1886 15 May: Dickinson dies of Bright's disease (a kidney disorder), or of hypertension
1890 First edition of Dickinson's poems, edited by Thomas Higginson and Mabel Loomis Todd, published

Historical, literary and social chronology

1798 Wordsworth and Coleridge's *Lyrical Ballads* published, launching the Romantic movement in England
1818 Mary Shelley's novel *Frankenstein* published
1819 John Keats's most productive year, in which he wrote many of his Odes
1831 Slave rebellion in Virginia, led by Nat Turner
1832 Andrew Jackson, Democrat, re-elected President of the US
1833 Ralph Waldo Emerson travels to Europe and meets Thomas Carlyle, Wordsworth and Coleridge
1834 Anti-Catholic demonstrations lead to Charlestown being burned
1836 Emerson's *Nature* published
1837 Carlyle's *The French Revolution* published; Queen Victoria crowned
1841 Carlyle's *On Heroes, Hero-Worship and the Heroic in History* published

1845 Edgar Allan Poe's *The Raven and Other Poems* published; the Irish potato famine begins, to last until 1850
1847 Emily Brontë's *Wuthering Heights* published; Charlotte Brontë's *Jane Eyre* published
1848 Walt Whitman's *The Leaves of Grass* published; first Women's Rights Convention held in New York; Californian Gold Rush begins; in Europe, revolutions in Italy, France and Germany; in England the pre-Raphaelite Brotherhood is formed
1850 Nathaniel Hawthorne's novel *The Scarlet Letter* published; the Compromise Bill in America restricts slavery in the territories; Wordsworth dies; Elizabeth Barrett Browning's political poem *The Runaway Slave at Pilgrim's Point* published
1852 Elizabeth Barrett Browning's *Sonnets from the Portuguese* published; Harriet Beecher Stowe's *Uncle Tom's Cabin* published
1854 Henry David Thoreau's *Walden* published
1855 Alfred Lord Tennyson's *Maud and Other Poems* published
1856 Elizabeth Barrett Browning's *Aurora Leigh*, a feminist poem, published
1860 Abraham Lincoln, Republican, elected President of the US
1861 American Civil War breaks out
1862 Christina Rossetti's *Goblin Market* published
1863 Lincoln proclaims the emancipation of the slaves; major battles in the Civil War
1865 Civil War ends when the Confederates surrender to General Lee; Lincoln assassinated
1866 Ku Klux Kan formed to protect the interests of the white population in the southern states of America
1868 Louisa May Alcott's *Little Women* published
1871 George Eliot's *Middlemarch* published
1881 Carlyle dies

Further Reading

Editions of Emily Dickinson's poems and letters

Martha Dickinson Bianchi (ed.), *The Single Hound: Poems of a Lifetime* (Little Brown, 1914)
R.W. Franklin (ed.), *The Manuscript Books of Emily Dickinson*, 2 vols. (Harvard University Press, 1981)
R.W. Franklin (ed.), *The Poems of Emily Dickinson: Variorum Edition*, 3 vols. (Harvard University Press, 1998)
Thomas H. Johnson (ed.), *The Poems of Emily Dickinson Including Variant Readings Critically Compared with All Known Manuscripts* (Harvard University Press, 1955)
Thomas H. Johnson (ed.), *The Complete Poems of Emily Dickinson* (Little Brown, 1960)
Thomas H. Johnson (ed.), *Emily Dickinson: Selected Letters* (Harvard University Press, 1971)
Thomas H. Johnson and Theodore Ward (eds.), *The Letters of Emily Dickinson*, 3 vols. (Harvard University Press, 1958)
Mabel Loomis Todd and T.W. Higginson (eds.), *Poems of Emily Dickinson* (Roberts Brothers, 1890)
Mabel Loomis Todd and Millicent Todd Bingham (eds.), *Bolts of Melody, New Poems by Emily Dickinson* (Harper & Brothers, 1945)

Biography

Richard B. Sewell, *The Life of Emily Dickinson*, 2 vols. (Farrar, Strauss and Giroux, 1974)

Critical books

Richard Chase, *Emily Dickinson* (William Sloane, 1951)
Joanne Feir Diehl, *Dickinson and the Romantic Imagination* (Princeton University Press, 1981)

Sandra M. Gilbert and Susan Gubar, *The Madwoman in the Attic: The Woman Writer and the Nineteenth-Century Literary Imagination* (Yale University Press, 1979)
Margaret Homans, *Bearing the Word: Language and Female Experience in Nineteenth-Century Women's Writing* (University of Chicago Press, 1989)
Susan Howe, *The Birthmark: Unsettling the Wilderness in American Literary History* (University Press of New England, 1993)
Suzanne Juhasz, *The Undiscovered Continent: Emily Dickinson and the Space of the Mind* (Indiana University Press, 1983)
Suzanne Juhasz (ed.), *Feminist Critics Read Emily Dickinson* (Indiana University Press, 1983)
Suzanne Juhasz, Cristanne Miller and Martha Nell Smith, *Comic Power in Emily Dickinson* (University of Texas Press, 1993)
Mary Loeffelholz, *Dickinson and the Boundaries of Feminist Theory* (Cambridge University Press, 1991)
Wendy Martin (ed.), *The Cambridge Companion to Emily Dickinson* (Cambridge University Press, 2002)
Helen McNeil, *Emily Dickinson* (Virago, 1986)
Cristanne Miller, *Emily Dickinson: A Poet's Grammar* (Harvard University Press, 1987)
Elizabeth Phillips, *Emily Dickinson: Personae and Performance* (Pennsylvania State University Press, 1988)
Vivian R. Pollak (ed.), *A Historical Guide to Emily Dickinson*, (Oxford University Press, 2004)
Barton Levi St Armand, *Emily Dickinson and Her Culture: The Soul's Society* (Cambridge University Press, 1984)
Daneen Wardrop, *Emily Dickinson's Gothic: Goblin with a Gauge* (University of Iowa Press, 1996)

Glossary

alliteration a sequence of words that use the same consonant sound (usually at the beginnings of words), for example *Success is counted sweetest* (see also **consonance**)
ambiguity where there are two or more meanings to a word or group of words, or a whole poem
analogy a literary comparison such as that in *'It was not Death, for I stood up'* where the speaker's feelings are compared to *Frost* and *Fire*
anaphora the deliberate repetition of words, as with *treading* in *'I Felt a Funeral, in my Brain'*
antithesis a contrast of ideas presented by strongly contrasted words, as in *She rose to His Requirement – dropt*
aphorism the concise expression of a generally accepted truth
apostles the close followers and disciples of Jesus, sent forth to preach, including Peter, Matthew, James and John
archetype a prototype or original model, such as the idea that God might represent the original and perfect Puritan
assonance a similarity or identity between the stressed vowels of two or more words, for example, *Wife*, *divine* and *mine* in *'Title divine – is mine!'*
aural something heard or representing the quality of being heard

bathos a movement from the sublime to the ridiculous, as in the satire on the ladies in *'What Soft – Cherubic Creatures'*, who at first are described perhaps as heavenly, but then are compared to a common, soft fabric: *Plush*

caesura a break between words in a metrical measure which is used to create particular effects, as in *Wild Nights – Wild Nights!*
closure an ending given to some of the poems, usually indicated by a full stop, which creates a sense of completeness
colloquialism an example of everyday language
common metre the metre or rhythm of hymns and ballads, consisting of four-line stanzas alternating between eight and six syllables per line, and generally rhyming *abab* or *abcb*
conceit a far-fetched comparison in which the reader is made to

admit likeness between two things while always being aware of the oddness of the comparison

conformist a person who abides by the rules of an institution, such as the Puritans' faith in their religion and its rules

consonance where words use the same sequence of consonants but with a change in the separating vowels, e.g. 'tip top' (see also **alliteration**)

cordial in medical terms a mixture that gives strength to the heart; also used as an adjective to mean warm, heartfelt or cheering

dialect a form of language related to a particular class or place, which has distinctive vocabulary and grammar

dramatic irony an effect created when a reader or an audience is aware of a situation, and a character in a poem/drama is not

dramatic monologue a form of poetry in which a single persona (created by the author) speaks to the reader, as in *'I'm "wife" – I've finished that'*

Elect those members of the Puritan religion who have been predestined for salvation

end-stopped a line of poetry that is drawn to a close by punctuation, as in *I'm Nobody! Who are you?*

enjambment where lines or stanzas in a poem run on to the next without a break in sense or punctuation, as in *He fumbles at your Soul/As Players at the Keys*

existentialism a philosophy made popular by Jean-Paul Sartre in the mid-twentieth century, according to which each person must choose his or her own route in life; this led to an idea of the pleasures of the 'here and now' being important to self-fulfilment, often the joys gained through the senses

Fall of Man the Christian doctrine according to which mankind lost the joys of paradise through the original sin of pride, which led to disobedience of God

feminine rhyme a rhyme that occurs in words of two or more syllables when the final syllable or syllables are not stressed, such as the rhyme of *formerly* with *Bee* in *'Did the Harebell loose her girdle'*

feminist criticism a school of criticism that aims to counteract male dominance in society and culture, and to view things from a female perspective

genre a type or form of literature, as in the Gothic genre, which Dickinson uses in '*One need not be a Chamber – to be Haunted*'

Gothic a type of literature developed at the end of the eighteenth century, typified by Mary Shelley's *Frankenstein*, in which there are supernatural events, terror, darkness, often a medieval setting, suspense, darkness and a female victim

half-rhyme a rhyme that is inexact, but sounds similar, as in *today/Victory* in '*Success is counted sweetest*'

Holy Spirit the third person of the Trinity of God the Father, God the Son (or Jesus Christ), and God the Holy Spirit (or Holy Ghost or Paraclete)

homonym a word that sounds the same as another word but is spelt differently. This device is used to great effect in the play between *I* and *eye* in '*Before I got my eye put out*'

iambic metre a metre consisting mainly of the pattern where one unstressed syllable is followed by one stressed syllable, as in *There came a Day at Summer's full*

imagery figurative language in literature, such as similes and metaphors, which appeals to the reader's senses or intelligence and extends the significance of a word

imperative verb the part of the verb that issues commands, as in '*Come slowly – Eden!*'

irony an effect achieved when words or actions carry a meaning apparently opposite from that intended, as in the irony of the bird table in '*Victory comes late*'

lyric a personal, song-like poem generally expressing emotion, such as '*Come slowly – Eden!*'

Marxism theories which follow the doctrines of Karl Marx (1818–1883), in which there is a belief that social change is driven by conflict between the classes, between the 'haves' and the 'have-nots'

masculine rhyme an exact, one-syllable, stressed rhyme, usually at the ends of lines, as in *Life/Wife* in '*She rose to His Requirement – dropt*'

metaphor a literary image in which one thing is seen to take on the characteristics of another, as when the *Harebell* looses her girdle, and human dress is applied to a flower

metaphysical a term used to define the poetry of a group of seventeenth-century writers led by John Donne, characterized by the use of far-fetched imagery and witty conceits; Dickinson displays this in some of her poems such as *''Twas like a Maelstrom, with a notch'*

metonym a figure of speech in which a characteristic or attribute of a thing is used to represent the whole thing, as the *Flag* is used in *'Step lightly on this narrow spot'*; a device that creates compression

metre the rhythm of a poem, which arises from the stress patterns

motif a recurring and important idea in a piece of literature, or group of poems, such as Dickinson's concern for the role of women in marriage

mutability the essential characteristic of change throughout life, which cannot be avoided; usually this is seen to lead to decay, as in *'Further in Summer than the Birds'*

narrative a poem that tells a story, such as *'Again – his voice is at the door'*

natural universe the world of nature as opposed to the world of human beings

onomatopoeia the effect when words sound like the thing they describe, as in the word *buzz*

orthodox conforming to the accepted norm, for example of the Puritan religion, or the role of women in marriage

Paraclete see **Holy Spirit**

paradox a self-contradictory statement or series of statements, evident in *'I cannot live with You'*

parody an imitation of a particular idea in a particular style in order to ridicule it, as in *'This World is not Conclusion'*

pathetic fallacy ascribing human emotions to non-human things, such as the weather in *'Wild Nights – Wild Nights!'*

patriarchy a male-dominated society

persona the speaker of a poem or a dramatic monologue

personification a literary device in which things or abstract ideas are treated as if they were human, as in the image of the bee getting drunk in *'I taste a liquor never brewed'*

psychoanalytic criticism the theory that behaviour and writings are influenced by deeply hidden psychological urges, made popular by Sigmund Freud at the turn of the nineteenth century

redemption the belief that Jesus died on the cross to redeem mankind from original sin, so that believers could be saved
register words and expressions appropriate to specific circumstances, such as the language of war in *'Step lightly on this narrow spot'*
resurrection life after death, and specifically the belief that Jesus, after lying in the tomb for three days, ascended to heaven
riddle the deliberate creation of a puzzle in words, as in *'I like to see it lap the Miles'*
Romantic movement a literary and philosophical movement of the beginning of the nineteenth century, often said to be led by Wordsworth and Coleridge, which valued emotion over reason, believed in the importance of self-exploration and perceived nature as a valuable teacher

sacrament an action ordained for Christians to follow in order to gain grace and achieve a place in heaven; Catholics believe in seven and Puritans in two: baptism and marriage
satire a work in which the aim is to teach or correct by means of irony and ridicule, as in *'What Soft – Cherubic Creatures'*
Seal in Puritan belief, the visible evidence of a promise made, such as the sacraments, which are a pledge of God's concern for mankind
secular non-religious; Dickinson takes away the theological meaning of salvation as being with God in heaven and applies it to being with her lover, as in *'There came a Day at Summer's full'*
sensory of the senses or sensations
sensual appealing to the senses or sensations, usually with a sexual implication, as in *'Did the Harebell loose her girdle'*
sensuous appealing to the senses, but with no specific implication of sexual or fleshly pleasure, as in *'Further in Summer than the Birds'*
simile a comparison using 'as' or 'like'; for example the snake parts the grass *as with a Comb* in *'A narrow Fellow in the Grass'*
Socialist a person who believes in the state ownership of the means of production, distribution, and exchange
stanza a verse of a poem
subjunctive mood the conjugation of a verb when it is conditional and the word 'if' is used or understood, as in *'Did the Harebell loose her girdle'*, where *Did* is in the subjunctive mood
sublime having a quality of grandeur which inspires awe

synaesthesia the mixing up of sense impressions, as when hearing and touch are conflated in the opening of *'There's a certain Slant of light'*

synecdoche a figure of speech in which a part is used to express the whole thing or person, as in the *hands* and *faces* in stanza 5 of *'There came a Day at Summer's full'*

syntax the order of words within a sentence; Dickinson often deliberately departs from normal syntax to create meanings, as in the last stanza of *'A Spider sewed at Night'*

tactile connected to the sense of touch, as in the imagery of the wind crawling on the skin in *'It was not Death, for I stood up'*

tenor that part of a metaphor which carries the meaning, as opposed to the image itself, which is the vehicle

Transcendental deriving from the theories of Ralph Waldo Emerson, which implied that people may surpass or transcend normal human experience by uniting with nature

Trinity see **Holy Spirit**

trope a literary figure or image, or part of a language register attached to a particular thing or idea, such as the religious imagery in *'There came a Day at Summer's full'*

'ubi sunt' a type of poetry originally Anglo-Saxon or Old English, in which the poet develops the idea of 'Where are they now?', in lament for past values which are now lost; used in Dickinson's *'Those – dying then'*

Unitarian a member of the church which believes that God has only one form, denying the existence of the Trinity

visionary a prophet or seer, as Dickinson believes the poet might claim to be in *'I dwell in Possibility'*

wit in literature a clever and unusual way of expressing something, such as the opening image in *'Before I got my eye put out'*

Appendix

Contexts in Emily Dickinson's poetry

The following list shows the contexts discussed in this book and the poems that may be relevant to each. Many of these contexts evidently overlap, and others will open up to the reader as familiarity with Dickinson's poems develops.

War/politics: 67, 444, 690, 754, 1183, 1551

Satires and comments upon society: 288, 401, 585

Love and sex: 211, 213, 249, 322, 446, 640, 663, 1670

Marriage: 199, 322, 528, 732, 1072, 1670

Death/immortality: 79, 216, 280, 465, 501, 712, 1100

Dramatic monologues and gender issues: 79, 199, 211, 213, 249, 327, 446, 465, 663, 712, 1072

Nature: 258, 328, 668, 986, 1068, 1286

Religion: 79, 315, 501

Definition/mental trauma: 254, 280, 341, 414, 510, 512

Psychological experience/personal values: 211, 213, 214, 258, 303, 327, 501, 512, 657, 670, 709, 747, 754, 1068, 1072, 1129, 1138, 1551, 1670

Poems about writing poetry: 441, 528, 657, 709, 741, 754, 1129, 1138, 1263, 1286, 1670